The Emerald Path

Maryfrances G. Botkin

Cover design by CreateSpace™

First Edition

Printed in the United States of America.

ISBN: 0615817378
ISBN-13: 978-0615817378

In loving memory of Philip Myron Scafe.

ACKNOWLEDGMENTS

I am deeply thankful to Donna Mortensen for her enormous wisdom and gentle prods of encouragement. Her endless enthusiasm for this project is what motivated me the most. Without her, this book could never have been written. Thank you, Bestie! Long live the Oxford comma!

Heartfelt thanks to Karen Polacheck for reading the book and giving me assistance, encouragement, and support that only a kindred-spirit can give. ILY

Thank you, Kristen Beno. No regrets.

Many thanks to Bonnie Pleisch for her amazing patience and kindness.

To my lovely editor and soul sister Bernadette Gambino for her loving support, guidance, and for proofing and editing endless submissions, and for always being there. Smink.

To my family, who suffered through mundane late-night suppers and piles of forgotten laundry. Most of all, for their love and support. Thank you!

And, finally, to NaNoWriMo - National November Writing Month. You helped me to discover the writer in me, and I never knew she even existed. Thank you.

For Ma & Dad, with all of my heart.
And to Rob … I still do.

If you want your children to be intelligent, read them Faerie tales. If you want them to be more intelligent, read them more Faerie tales.
~ Albert Einstein

Part One

1

Lila put down her sketchpad. Usually sketching was a stress reliever for her. Not tonight. She looked down at her drawing. Shaking her head, she frowned and squinted, turning her head. *Sometimes, stuff really did look better when you squinted.* It worked; it was beautiful. The only problem was, most people didn't have to squint to see and appreciate art, and chances were that if they had to, it sucked. Frustrated, she picked up the pad and closed it, putting her pencils back into the old salsa jar and placing it onto the little round table by her kitchen window. That was where she did most of her drawing, in the kitchen, and usually late in the evenings. The night allowed creativity to be snarky and naughty, though there were no curfews where art was concerned. It seemed right at night and she liked where it took her.

Now, she was tired and fighting another headache. Taking two Tylenol, she threw them into her mouth and swallowed them down, grimacing as last of her now-cold tea eased them down her throat. Turning out the kitchen light, she did her usual rounds of securing her tiny house. She lived alone and, quite frankly, liked being alone at least for the time being. Her fiancée, Roan, was in Ireland. His brother, Ethan, had just passed away after a horrible and long battle with cancer. Roan begged Lila to come with him. She simply could not go. Work would not allow it. But, as badly as she felt not being with him in his time of deep sorrow, she felt a secret stab of relief. Not that she couldn't do what she wanted when Roan was around; she could. Still, a devilish taste of freedom gave her a bit of peace. Talk of wedding dresses, table-scapes and flowers was bluntly put on hold, and that pleased her immensely.

Lila Quinn. Born into a hard-working Irish-American family. Both parents were killed when she was just thirteen years old by a drunk driver on their way home from a New Year's Eve party. Being an only child, she was very close to them, and her world fell apart when they died. She was her father's shadow, and she never really came to terms with having to live the rest of her life without him. While she was also close to her mother, she never truly felt the same sort of bond that she had with her father. Still, there were times she ached for her; everyone needed mothering. She was sent to live with her older cousin in Maine. Lila had always been close to her cousin, and was grateful that she was to be a part of her family, in the truest sense.

Art flowed out of her body like the tears she cried for her father. Both of her parents were artists, so it just came natural to her. All throughout her academic career, her binders and notebooks were always covered in doodles and designs. Even the jeans and sneakers she wore were canvases for her. She knew she would always do something with art, but because she was not a good student, it was hard. She hated school. She did just enough to get by, and managed to graduate high school by the skin of her teeth. That's why now, she not only worked at a place she hated, in a position she that seemed beneath her, for people she had no respect for, but also why she was going to the community college: to better her life, and to somehow incorporate the one thing she loved into her professional life, art. That is where she met Roan Donovan.

2

Lila and Roan had hit it off immediately. Literally. Turning a corner in a hurry, her face smashed into his arm as she was turning to look for the bathrooms. He not only helped her gather her strewn papers, but showed her where the restrooms were. Normally, she would have taken her time to thank such a handsome guy for helping her, but when you have to pee as badly as she had had to, she simply gave him a nervous nod and ran like Hell for it. *Shit, I'll never see him again. Thank God, too.* She was wrong. She saw him again a few days later and he asked if she needed directions to the rest room again. She got a kick out of that. A really bad line, but she thought that was cool, and brave of him to ask. Still, the glint in his eye and the way his full lips curled when he smiled; he was devilishly handsome so why not? She swallowed her pride (and her gum) and asked him out.

They immediately hit it off and dated exclusively. It felt so good having a new friend, and the fact that he was amazing-looking only helped. Progressing to a physical relationship, it just seemed right. Soon, they were inseparable. Three years later, he proposed. There was no time for celebrating, though. Roan's brother, Ethan, was diagnosed with pancreatic cancer. Living alone in Ireland, Ethan was cared for by friends but longed for his brother. By the time Roan arrived in Dublin, Ethan had died. Lila cursed her employers. She longed to be with Roan. She knew he was hurting so deeply and that he would be alone in making all of the funeral arrangements.

She had absolutely no desire to put any kind of effort into work, but she had bills to pay. The tiny house had been the home of her late aunt. Her cousin was left the tiny house in her mother's will. Karen had already married and lived in Texas and had no use for it. She offered it to Lila, who accepted without question; she loved the little house. Now the house was hers, mortgage-free. She also received a little bit of inheritance money from her aunt and uncle. It wasn't a lot, but she could certainly manage without having to rely on ramen noodles for supper every night. Still, it was not enough for her to live on if she quit working. "It could always be worse," she said aloud as she turned off her lamp. She said a silent prayer, asking that Roan have an easy time and be kept safe safe, then went to sleep.

3

Wiping tears from her cheeks, Lila went into the kitchen and took out the wine from the small wine rack on the counter. Cheap Bordeaux. She removed the cork and poured a large glass. No wine glasses this time; this called for a tumbler. Sniffling, she tore a paper towel off of the roll and blew her nose. She then drank the wine in three large swallows. Gasping for air, she grimaced as the acrid liquid burned her throat. Still, she poured another half glass. Sipping now, she stared out of the kitchen window. It wasn't what one would call a fight, but it certainly wasn't an agreement either. Roan was having trouble getting Ethan's death certificate sorted out. That, combined with all of the normal stresses of dealing with putting a funeral together in a foreign land, grieving, and missing Lila, he was not fairing well. He missed her, terribly. He wanted her with him. She wanted the same but knew it simply could not happen and felt hopeless. They both hung up feeling torn apart. She wasn't a drinker really, but tonight if she couldn't have Roan, she'd at least have wine.

It was late now. Past midnight. She locked up and decided to do something she rarely ever did and watched some television. She pulled the crocheted afghan across her lap and flipped through the channels. Her head still spinning from the earlier wine, she blinked and tried to find something interesting to watch. She finally decided on a movie she was familiar with. She watched for a while then felt the first waves of sleepiness creeping in. She yawned. She felt her heavy lids falling. She fought to keep them open, shaking her head and it was then that out of the corner of her eye, she thought she saw something move. She blinked and looked to her right moving just her eyes. Fear crept in. She saw nothing. Leaning up, she rested her chin onto her hand and peered forward. Nothing. She sat up and forced herself to watch the television, pulling the afghan tightly around her. *It's the wine.* she mused sleepily. "Oh, fuck this." she said aloud and clicked the television off. Keeping the afghan wrapped tightly around her, she turned off the lamp. Turning out the bathroom light, she made her way down the hallway to her bedroom.

As she was just about to go in, she saw a flash. A tiny flash from around the corner toward the second bedroom. It looked like someone had just lit a match. The fear returned, hairs on her arms and neck sticking out. A white-hot cape of dread covered her body. This time she ran toward the unknown light. Fearing that her house may be on fire, she braced herself for something to come at her. Her feet, covered in thick socks, slid on the hardwood floor as she ran toward the closed door where the light had flickered. She nearly fell but managed to quickly open the door. The force of her pushing the old wooden door slammed it against the wall with a loud bang. No fire. No smoke. Nothing. "I know I saw that!" she said, again out loud to no one. She looked in the closet. Behind the door. She took a breath, bracing herself and looked in that most-feared place, under the bed. Again, nothing.

Now, for the first time, she felt like she was being watched. But by whom? By what? This was the one thing she hated about living alone, being frightened at night. Having searched the entire house and finding nothing, she helplessly called Roan. She didn't care if it was four in the morning in Ireland. He sleepily answered. She instantly felt stupid and suddenly was embarrassed. He laughed through a long yawn,

"Had a little wine, did we?" he joked. Instantly irritated, her reply was firm.

"No, it wasn't the wine, Roan! I swear I saw something!" He yawned again.

"Baby, if you're that sure you saw something and you think it was fire, call 911!" He no longer sounded sleepy, but angry. Now, she really felt stupid. The house would have been fully engulfed by now. She apologized, not only for waking him up, but for the way she had ended the previous conversation. The two of them blamed it all on stress. After a sweet goodnight message (and a reminder to do one more walk-through), she hung up the phone, feeling much better about things. Satisfied that nothing was burning or unlocked, she crept into her warm bed, pulling up the soft flannel sheets. Wrapping her legs around a pillow she wished was Roan, she hugged it close and drifted into a dreamless sleep.

4

It was very hard for her to see the Human from where she stood. Her back ached from the constant crouching and peering. She had no idea how she ended up here, and her growing fear was that she would not only forget where she came in, but that she was stuck here with no way out.

I have to get out of here, she said to herself.

Nyx is 31 years old. Her skin is a lovely shade of teal (unless she's ill and then she takes on a deep purple tinge), and she stands about 18 inches tall. Not a tiny Fae, but not the largest, either. As a child, she often wandered out of her allowed range to watch the Humans. She was fascinated by the giant people.

"Nyxie, their world is a very dangerous place for Fae. Never go there unless you are with me," warned her mother. She remembered stories, horrible stories that were told on long treks to the merchants village. It wasn't that the Humans were bad or evil, they were just so large! Everything they used was large, and being in the Human world could result in a painful death. In olden times, she remembered hearing her Grand-momma telling stories about the curious Fae children who went on adventures looking for the Humans, and how they never came home. One especially horrifying story told of an elfin boy who was burned to death by a flying smoldering object the Humans called, "cigarette." *Why would beings choose to suck smoke into their bodies? I hear it's something they do to relax? Why would they do that when it can only do harm?* Nyx always had wondered, and never understood, either. It disgusted her.

Because it was so very dark, Nyx could not make out her surroundings other than the stripes of bright light that came through the windows from the outdoor lights on the street. She was tired. She decided to slowly walk until she came to that area in the big room where she saw the Human reclining. There was a big tree in this room. She could climb it and find a branch to sleep on. She was used to that. When she went hunting with her father, they slept in trees all the time. This was a smaller tree than she was used to, but still, she could fly up. She looked around. No Humans. Her long wings illuminated a golden glow as she ascended into to the tree and disappeared into it, landing on a sturdy inner branch. She sat for a moment, her wings' glow ebbing as they folded like tissue paper behind her. She held on tightly, looking around for any sign of movement. Finally, convinced that there was nobody in the rooms and that the late hour meant that they were probably sleeping, she, exhausted from the day's travels, curled her tiny body into the crook of her branch, hugged herself and fell into a deep and much needed sleep.

5

Nyx's eyes popped open. There were sounds all around her. Humming. Water running. A woman singing. She clung to her leaf and pulled it close to her. A whoosh of air nearly blew her off of her branch and Nyx squeezed her eyes tightly shut in case she had to... what? Fly away? She relaxed. Heavy footsteps. She saw the Human. In the light of day she could now see that this Human was like herself, female. And beautiful. This Human liked to sing with her mouth shut. She watched as the Human went back into the room with the noise. She was drinking something black. *Ew, coffee*. Nyx shuddered. Soon, the Human picked up a brown bag and a bunch of metal objects that were attached to a ring. *Keys! Humans have keys, too!* She giggled then covered her mouth. In a flash, the Human was out the door. Nyxie soon heard a door slam and an engine roar. The noise faded. She took a deep breath. "Now, to find my way out of here!" she said to the tree.

6

Nyx eased her leg over the lip of the pot. She sat on the edge, catching her breath. She looked around the room as she picked off pieces of bark. The room looked entirely different in daylight. She looked down. She could have jumped, but she decided to just glide being so tired. Opening her silvery wings, she drifted down onto the carpeting. Folding her wings behind her, she began walking toward the hallway near the bedrooms. If she remembered correctly, her path ended somewhere along those planks in the flooring.

"This is the last time I ever do this. Stupid. Stupid!" she said aloud. As soon as she said it, she regretted it. She had no idea if there were any more Humans inside here. She clamped her mouth with her hand and listened, her big periwinkle eyes darting around. She heard nothing. Relaxing, she let out her breath. She began walking again. She reached the hallway, but it didn't seem right.

This wasn't the right way.

Panic began to set in. She cursed under her breath. Suddenly, she saw something white skirt across the floor in front of her. She sucked in her breath and dared herself not to scream. She bit her lip. The white thing was an animal. A cat! She knew cats! Knew of them, anyhow. She knew she should be very careful; this thing could have her for lunch in one swift lick. She waited and soon the cat went into another room, somewhere.

"I'm getting too old for this shit," she muttered angrily as she regained her composure. Looking along the floorboards, she noticed a crack. "That has to be it," she muttered. "That's it!" She knelt down in front of the crack on the floorboard next to the baseboard. Smiling, she recognized the baseboard because it was coming away from the wall. "That's where I came in!" She pulled the baseboard out just enough so she could squeeze through. Nyx let out an exhilarated yell and was gone.

7

Lila unlocked the front door and, pushing it open with her knee, all but dropped her grocery bags on the floor. "Ow," she said, looking at her red fingers sore from trying to lug all of the grocery bags in one trip. "At least I didn't drop anything." She took her coat off and threw her keys in the glass dish on the coffee table. She put her groceries away and then made a few phone calls. She was supposed to go bowling with some friends but was coming down with a cold. She cancelled her plans. It was chilly so she decided she'd build a fire and have some tomato soup for supper. She put her cell phone on to charge and then started gathering kindling. After she was satisfied with her fire, she made some soup and changed into her pajamas. She put on the Erik Satie CD that was sitting on the table. She was in a bad mood, and his music seemed to season it further. She sipped the hot soup, cradling the mug in her hands. As she stared into the fire; Satie's flippant notes took her mind off of the chill in her body. She wasn't looking to be cheered up. Sometimes she liked dark music and a dark mood.

Soon, though, her thoughts returned to Roan and how they had spent many nights in this very same spot, kissing and talking about their future. She sipped the last of her soup then, grabbing a box of tissues, settled onto the sofa with her sketchbook.

***

Nyx was lost after all. It was the right exit but now she didn't know where to go. She was sore, tired, and very hungry. The only thing to do would be to go back to the Human's home. *At least I'd be warm*, she thought aloud. Finally she found the familiar beam of light and crept back through the baseboard. An instant sense of warmth met her. As she climbed through, the aroma of something sweet filled her nostrils and she inhaled deeply. Letting her breath out, she looked around. While it was darker again, there was light to her left. She remembered the cat and just as she remembered, the cat was staring right at her. Nyx froze. The cat was beautiful; mostly white with pale blue eyes. It stopped in front of her. Nyx dared not move. The cat inched closer. Suddenly,

"Hitch? Whatcha see, boy? Got yourself another mouse, huh?" Nyx panicked. The cat let out a growl. "Come here, you bad boy," the Human said. "Let's go get you a treat." And at that, Hitch turned and ran and just as quickly, while Nyx darted as fast as she could back toward the baseboard. Loud vibrations told her the Human was coming. She slid behind the baseboard just in time and hid behind it. It was cold in there. Fear and the temperature made her shiver madly.

I can't stay in here all night. Nyx thought. When she heard the Human making noise in the kitchen, she made a run for it. She ran until she was away from the wall then arched her tiny body and flew straight up. She flew as fast as her wings could carry her and when she came to the end of the hall, her body zipped to the left. Seeing that she was about to hit a giant bed head on, she lowered herself and darted under it. She hit something soft and furry. Fearing it was another cat, she let out a tiny "EEP!" Only this cat didn't move. It wasn't a cat at all. It was a shoe. A blue slipper. She stood up and leaned against it, brushing the fur away from her sweaty face, trying to catch her breath. Her tiny breasts heaving, she let her head fall onto the side. As soon as she caught her breath, she listened. Again, hearing that the Human was still far away in another room, she let her guard down and opened her wings; instead of turning gold when she flew, they turned a deep shade of cobalt blue. She fanned herself. As she cooled off, her wings changed color again. This time, a soft white glow illuminated the area. A pair of slippers lay just by the bed. In the middle of the area was the mate of the blue slipper. She went under the bed toward it. It was covered in dust. Her nose scrunched up in disgust and she had to fight to not sneeze. She looked at the pair by the bed's edge. Pink and fluffy and clean.

No dust, either, she thought. It was light, too. She pushed a pink slipper toward the middle of the area under the bed, and pushed the blue dusty one next to the pink one. *Maybe she won't notice.* She knew that was a risky thing to think. "I'll just make sure I switch them back before she goes to bed." She then climbed inside the pink slipper and fell straight to sleep.

8

Lila yawned. Scribbling down notes, she tried to concentrate on her instructor's lecture. Usually she enjoyed this class. Art History. Tonight's discussion: Formal Analysis. She had a huge paper coming up and needed to choose a period (early Macedonian) and two pieces by two different artists and compare style, materials used, similarities and differences. This would be a breeze for her. Still, she was so sleepy. She stayed until she had the most important information, then left. She still didn't feel well, either. All she could think about was sitting in a hot tub of water, sipping more soup and Nyquil. It was when she arrived on her street that her stomach lurched. It was all she could to not to vomit in the car. Fumbling through her keys, she finally found the house key and jammed it into the lock, left the door open and ran into the bathroom. She purged for five minutes. Beads of sweat dripped off her bangs and her ribs felt as if they could crack from the force. Feeling that she could finally stand, she flushed the toilet and rinsed out her mouth. She was shaking.

"Oh, shit," she said aloud to her reflection. Feeling Hitch rub against leg she relaxed. "Cat, I feel like shit. Go feed yourself." Hitch only purred louder. "Oh, Goddammit. Alright," she moaned. Still uneasy, she slowly trod to the kitchen and fed the cat, though the smell of the cat food nearly set her stomach off again. She also put the kettle on for tea. She didn't want it but knew she had to keep hydrated. Taking the tea into her bedroom, she set it on her nightstand where it was ignored for the rest of the night. Pulling the comforter and sheets tightly around her chilled body, Lila fell into a fitful sleep.

***

The noise of the door being unlocked jolted Nyx awake. She had awakened earlier, but was still so tired that she instantly fell back to sleep. Now noises were everywhere. Keys, running. Then that awful sound of sick. It kept going on and on! Nyx instantly felt sorry for the Human. Finally the sick stopped. Footsteps and then more footsteps. Closer. She heard the clink of china on the nearby table followed by loud squeaks. A ruffle of the bedclothes being shuffled. Finally a loud, "Uuuugh." The only sound now was the angry growl of the Human's stomach, and an occasional snore. Instantly, Nyx felt better. Now, she could try to find something to eat. Just as she was about to climb out of the slipper, the cat came in. She could see it from where she was. She watched it as it licked a paw, then it jumped up onto the bed. She waited. Silence. She silently crawled out. Curiosity filled her. She crawled up the leg of the nightstand. Reaching the top, she pulled herself up, using her wings to steady her. The Human's face was so close! She was sleeping, but her hair was wet. Her mouth was open and her breath was like spoiled fire. It made Nyx grimace. Pulling herself up a bit higher, she saw that the cat was curled into a white ball, fast asleep at the Human's feet. Deciding she didn't want to climb, she expanded her silver wings wider and in an instant, she was out in the hallway. She flew into the kitchen. Landing on the counter by the sink, she jumped in. A drop of water lay in a perfect bead. She tasted it. It was glorious. She drank the droplet away. Another one fell. It scared her, splashing her. She flew away, her tiny heart beating out of her tiny chest. Wiping her wet blue-black hair away from her eyes, she suddenly giggled. Seeing a huge bowl of fruit on the dining room table, she soared to it. She had no way to peel the big yellow one, or the pretty orange one. The big purple ones, she could manage. She kicked a grape with all of her might and it split open. She ate heartily. Back to the sink again. She washed her hands in the beads of water, this time keeping an eye on the faucet and leaping out of the way of the cold water when it fell.

Refreshed and satisfied, Nyx could now concentrate on finding her way home. She missed her circle and had chores to attend to. Stumbling into this world was an accident, and while it fascinated her, she had to get home. She flew back to the hallway and landed just outside the now misplaced baseboard. She squeezed behind it and then back inside the darkness. She illuminated her wings. Now she could take her time and rethink her steps. She crept along a dusty plank. Huge spiders hung. Spiders were okay. She was familiar with them. Being an Earth Fae, she was familiar with just about all creatures, and knew how to speak to them. English was familiar, too. It was heard all over. Her world was lush and green, but it was also very near the Human world, so language was easily learned. Fae knew just about every language, depending on where they lived.

She walked for what seemed like hours. Finally seeing the familiar door, she flew toward it. It was a tiny round door. She opened it and was immediately awash with the familiar scents of home. She flew until she came to her area of home. She lived in a holly bush. The poisonous berries kept most predators away. She flew past her bush and landed near the brook. She stepped into the warm water and bathed. It felt wonderful. She then lay in the sun and dried off for a bit and flew back home. Sitting on a twig, she started thinking about the Human. The sick Human. She had never ever seen a one so close up before. Lots of her friends had their Human homes. She never felt the need to find one; if it was meant to be, it would happen. *Why go out of my way to try to find one that might like me?*

Technically speaking, Nyx was a Pixie. Most pixies were troublemakers and liked to pull pranks on Humans. Nyx was sometimes embarrassed for them. It just seemed so stupid to keep going back and playing dumb jokes on Humans. While she did have friends, she only had a few true friends. She was a loner Fae. Thinking about the Human, she began wondering if perhaps it might be nice to have a household to visit. One that would hopefully welcome her and let her come and go as she pleased. But only if the Human wanted it. Some Humans only wanted to contact Fae for a price, to gain money. Money was something the Fae truly did not understand. If they needed, they received. Everyone did for each other. It was just the way they lived. Money seemed, to Fae, to only make others angry and greedy. Their way of life was so much simpler.

Nyx considered the sick Human. She didn't even know her name. She remembered the cat's name. Hitch. Hitch with the light blue eyes. Her gaze went to the ground where she focused on the dewy grass and the glittery path that led to her bush. As her eyes grew heavy, the glittery green path faded from her view, and her path of Fae dust was forgotten.

9

Lila stretched. Hitch stretched as well, arching his back and extending his white legs. He then crept up to Lila, who scratched his ears. Hitch turned his head in ecstasy and plopped down beside her. Her stomach hurt. She wasn't feeling as sick as she had earlier, but she knew she was still not well. She slowly sat up and sure enough, pangs of pain squeezed her stomach. She grabbed her cell phone and called her boss. She'd be missing class, too. She didn't care. She felt lousy. Standing up, her foot fumbled under the bed for her slippers. She slid her foot in and then slid the other into the one next to it. They didn't match. She kicked the blue one off and tried to find the matching pink one with her foot. "Dammit. Where is it?" She finally had to kneel down and look. "What the hell is it doing way back there?" She grabbed it and threw it onto the floor. "Damn cat." Slipping it on, she went to the bathroom.

She went back to her bedroom and fetched the now ice-cold tea by her bedside. She went into the kitchen. Her eyes hurt. *I must*

have a fever, she thought "Kitty, I'm staying here with you today."
She poured the cold tea down the sink and rinsed her cup out. It
was then that a tiny sparkle caught her eye. It looked like very fine
greenish glitter all over the bottom of the sink. She ran her finger
through it. When she looked at it, she noticed that the same stuff
was all over her hand. Puzzled, she rubbed her finger and thumb
together and looked again. "What the hell?" She shrugged it off
and washed her hands. "I need a shower, Hitch. Out of my way."
She thought nothing of the substance on her fingers. It wasn't
sticky or wet. In the hallway, something caught her eye. "What *is*
that?" A very thin line of fine green glitter went down the hallway
and then divided into both bedrooms. She was now a bit
concerned. She turned and sure enough, there was an even wider
path near the baseboards. "Mice don't wear glitter."

She knelt down and looked at the path. She touched it. It stuck
to her index finger. She ran into the bathroom and turned on the
light. In the brighter light, the dust turned iridescent blues, greens,
purples, and yellows. It was stunning. It was beautiful. It was
weird. It didn't feel like anything. It wasn't glitter; not even the
finest glitter Martha Stewart sold. She tried to think of a word to
describe it. She couldn't. As she tried to get an even closer look, it
began to disappear. "What the fuck!?" Now she was freaked out.
She stood up and ran back into the hallway. The green dust was
gone. "Okay. I am feverish. I am sick. None of this is real. I need a
shower – and a shrink."

Later that afternoon she called Roan. This time it was Lila who
needed to hear his voice. She explained how sick she was and told
him of the odd dust. He laughed it off. "Babe, you need a hot
toddy. Try to sleep. I'm sorry you're so sick. I miss you so much."

Her stomach turned at the thought of alcohol. "Ew. No, I just want some broth. I can't seem to get warm." Roan's demeanor changed at this confession.

"Go to the doctor, Lila. You could be getting dehydrated. Be sure to keep drinking; get some Gatorade."

She agreed, though the thought of going out made her shiver even harder. She decided to call her neighbor and see if she could stop by the store on the way home from work. "Of course! Let me know what you need. I can make you a batch of my famous chicken soup," Erin said. Lila hung up, grateful for good friends. She took a shower then put on some comfortable yoga pants and her Redskins sweatshirt. Grabbing the blanket off of the rocking chair, she was about to head to the sofa when she noticed more green glittery dust on her ficus tree. She looked at it, turning her head sideways. Shivering, she pulled the blanket around her and shook her head.

"I can't do this now. Sleep...need to sleep."

As she turned toward the couch, the green dust disappeared. Lila didn't notice. Fever overtook her and she fell into a deep sleep, Hitch warming her feet.

10

Nyx threw the dead leaves into the marsh. She then gathered her flowers and herbs and walked home. It was a long walk, but it felt good. While she was very glad to be home, her mind kept returning to the sick Human. She quickened her pace. She was suddenly joined by two more Fae. They greeted her happily as they flew by her side and offered to help carry her load. She gratefully accepted.

"Where were you? We came for our tea the other day, but you were gone. What happened?" Alva, also a pixie, landed in step with Nyx and took her bundle of wildflowers.

"I got a bit lost," she said, dejectedly, "in the *other* world." Nyx could hear the collective gasps. Alva stopped in her tracks. The other faerie, Drake, also stopped.

"You? Lost? Well, well. What do you think about that, Alva? She finally did it!" Nyx, now irked, shook her head in annoyance. Drake patted Nyx on the shoulder. "Forgive me, Love; I'm just glad that you are finally starting to spread your wings, in the most literal sense, my friend." Nyx stopped and hugged him.

"Forgiven. It was so strange, though. I found this Human...I keep thinking about her. She's young, like us. She's also ill. I can't stop thinking about her." She continued the story of her adventure the entire walk home. Her friends were thrilled for her.

"You should go back! This could be your chance to have a house! And, if your Human befriends you, your own entrance, too," Alva said excitedly. Nyx smiled. "Or, it could end up being vary unsafe." Alva added. Nyx ignored her. She remembered how warm the Human's home was, how nice it smelled. It was cozy. Inviting.

"It was nice. Still, I was afraid that I would not find my way home so I really didn't explore much. I slept when I had the chance. I ate when it was safe." Drake sat at the base of Nyx's tree. Drake was a Water Sprite who lived on edge of the pond a mile away from Nyx's holly bush. Most water sprites don't wear clothing, but Drake *loved* clothes and though he was a round, fat Sprite, he was still extremely handsome. He made all of his own clothing, using vibrant colors and fabrics. He loved watching flamboyant young Human men in their dashing colors and suits. His black hair always tousled. Deep blue eyes completed his look. Handsome and wild.

"Go back. We can tell you how to proceed. Many Fae wish to have a second home in a Human house." His voice grew louder as Nyx flew her items up into her bush. "They become a part of the family. It's rare but it does happen." Drake's thick Irish voice pealed with excitement. Nyx sat beside him. Alva chimed in.

"It's dangerous! I mean, you could risk being exposed. Humans can be mean, and just want to expose us. Can you imagine what would happen to us, Drake?" Alva continued as she joined them on the mossy floor. Like Nyx, Alva was a pixie. Never had anyone seen such a nervous pixie. Alva was a worrier. Nyx and Drake often said that Alva worried enough for the three of them.

"I have an aunt and uncle that found a Human family and lived with them for over thirty years. It was the wife who found them in their tool shed. It took her six years to convince her husband that they were really there. Once he did actually see them, he grew so excited, but also wanted to show the world. She begged him not to expose them. Over time, he grew to care about them as well and promised to never photograph or endanger them. The Humans had a son, but he never had contact. He was a bad kid. His parents were afraid of how he would react if he knew they were there. The Humans hid my aunt and uncle from him. He was killed in a car accident just after he left for college. Their grief was for the child that could have been, not for the person he was. It was very sad. I heard heartsick stories from them.

"Slowly, the Humans coaxed them from out of hiding and even built them a little house to live in up in the attic. I wish I could have seen it. It sounded so sweet. But, it's rare to find that, Nyxie." Alva shook her head. "I'm not sure I like this," she confessed.

To Nyx, it suddenly sounded perfect. Silently she decided she would find her way back. She'd mark her path this time.

"What is wrong with your Human?" Drake asked. Nyx sighed.

"She's not my Human." She shot an irritated glace at Drake, his eyes smiled though his lips did not. "I don't know. She seemed very feverish. A lot of vomiting and ague. She wants to sleep a lot.

She has stress. She misses her lover. He is in Ireland." Drake's interest piqued when she said this. As she spoke, she noted herbs she could quickly gather to make a healing tea. Alva read her face.

"Nyx, go back. At least make her a brew for her fever and vomiting. Watch her. Make sure she recovers, and that it's nothing more than fever and ague. She's alone, right?" Drake stood, frowning, wiping wet moss off of his backside.

"We'll help you gather supplies. Yes, go. You'll have a better sense of her after you stay for a few days. We will travel with you and help you set up a temporary resting place in her wall. You'll be comfortable," he said as he hugged her. He kissed her forehead. "What's the worst that can happen?" he said with a smile as he flew up into her holly bush.

"I become catnip for Hitch," she whispered to nobody.

11

Lila pulled her thick robe snugly around her. Shivering, she sat in her kitchen. She watched her neighbor, Erin, stirring a pot of simmering soup. Though it smelled wonderful, her stomach had other ideas.

"I'll just get it to the boil then I'll turn it off. It'll stay hot for hours. I put some Gatorades in the fridge, too. You have to stay hydrated, Lila." She turned to face Lila. "Let me take your temperature. Where...?" Lila nodded toward the hall.

"Bathroom. Medicine chest," she said between shivers. She had never felt so cold in all of her life. That meant, of course, that she was probably burning up. Erin returned and washed the thermometer, shook it, then briskly shoved it into Lila's mouth.

"Under the tongue. If you are above 101°, I'm taking you to the hospital." The thought of leaving her warm house scared her and made her shiver all the more.

"N-no. I'll be okay h-here. Please. Don't m-make me g-go outs-side." Lila began coughing. Erin felt Lila's head.

"Stop talking. Close your mouth so it'll register." Erin pulled a chair closer and sat facing Lila. She rubbed Lila's arms briskly in an effort to warm her. Lila's eyes closed. Her head fell back. She could have fallen asleep this way, but she brought her head back up. Erin removed the thermometer. "God. 103°. That's that. Let's get you dressed." Lila began sobbing and it made her chest burn.

"No. Please! It's so cold outside. I c-can't ..." Erin knelt down in front of Lila, brushing fallen hair away from Lila's face.

"Lila. You have to go. I'll be with you, and you'll be warm. You either go with me, or I call an ambulance." Erin looked sternly at her. "Your choice. I'll make sure you're warm. Now, where is your purse? You'll need your insurance card."

Lila allowed Erin to dress her. Lila protested in anguish as Erin removed her robe. Lila's teeth chattered so hard she thought her teeth would crack. It was agonizing waiting for Erin to shove a sweatshirt on her. Lila put her robe back on and let Erin put slippers over her heavily socked feet. She put the hood of her sweatshirt over her head and crossed her arms tightly across her body. Erin helped her to stand and once she was ready, slowly walked Lila outside. Her shivering increased. Erin helped her down the steps and across Lila's lawn to her own car. Lila never felt so sick in all of her life.

12

"I'm in what they call 'Fast Track,' Roan," Lila said calmly. "I have pneumonia. I ..." Before she could finish, Roan interrupted her.

"What? Did you say pneumonia? I'm coming home." Lila tried to speak. A fit of coughing stopped her. She had to put the phone down it was so bad. A nurse came in and told her to end her phone call and to stop talking immediately. Nodding and coughing, Lila agreed.

"Yes, Roan, pneumonia. No, you can't come home. D-don't come home. Look, I can't talk too long or I'll cough. I'll be going home in the morning. I need to sleep, Roan. Please. Can you hear me?" The nurse gave her a stern look. Lila nodded at her. "Okay," she whispered to her. The nurse left. "Roan, baby, I'll be fine. Erin is next door, and said she'd stay with me. Do you hear me, Roan? Roan?" The connection was bad.

"Yes, I heard you. Goddammit, I need to come home. I just – I can't now, Lila. I hate that you're so sick and that I can't be there to help you. I hate all of this shit." Roan's voice cracked. Lila could tell he was crying. "I guess we should be glad that you didn't come with me, after all, huh?" Lila coughed a little. She too was now crying. It hurt. For the first time, she truly felt how sick she was. Her chest felt full and heavy, her back hurt. "Baby, just rest. I'm not going to call you, but when you get home, call me. Just to let me know that you're there, okay? Lila, I'm praying for you. I love you so much." Tears ran down Lila's cheeks. She longed to have him there with her. Still, she put on a brave voice and reassured him that she would do nothing but rest.

"I promise. I'll call you tomorrow. I love you, Roan. So much." She ended the call and sobbed. She never saw the nurse reenter the room.

I think you could use a cup of tea," she said, unfolding a warm blanket. She covered Lila with it, tucking her in." I'll be back with some and your antibiotics." She smiled sweetly at her then checked her IV.

"Thank you," Lila said through tears. The warmth from the blanket felt so good and she snuggled into it." I want to cry, but it hurts." She blew her nose and had another coughing fit. Though her head felt as if it would explode, she suddenly had a sense of pure comfort. If Roan could not comfort her, this would do. She watched as the nurse left the room. She turned out the light and looked out the window at the night sky. A storm was coming. The sky lit up with distant lightening. Snuggling deeper into the warm blankets she finally felt safe. "I love you, Roan," she whispered to the night, eyes closing.

13

"There. See the light down there? On the left. That's it." Nyx led them to the portal where the she entered before. Traveling underground, it took hours. There were many paths and avenues to choose. Being a novice in this area, Nyx was quickly disoriented. Telling Drake and Alva the paths she followed previously made them laugh.

"You took the scenic route. There is a much easier way. It takes a lot longer, but it's basically a straight shot. From now on, take this route." As they neared the entrance, Nyx shushed them.

"Let's not do anything to scare her. All I really want to do right now is to make sure she is okay. If it means not meeting her for a year, then so be it. Her health must come first." Drake snorted.

"That's why we will set you up right here. A little nook. You can sleep here and eat here. We will make sure you are able to survive in here for a week. That should give you enough time to ... er ...

evaluate your Human." Nyx stopped unpacking. "I know, I know, she's not your Human. Yet."

Very quickly and very quietly, the three Fae set up Nyx's little home. "Until we can find something better, use the chamomile leaves for a bed. It's actually quite warm in here. You won't need bedclothes." Alva looked around. "Look! That board against the wall will make a great shelf!" She arranged the flowers and herbs along its top. "There. Not bad!" Stopping to survey her new temporary home, she suddenly realized how tired she was. Still, she had to find the Human. She had an odd feeling that Lila was sicker than she originally had thought. She stood and peered out of the baseboard.

"I'm making sure Hitch isn't around." Hearing her friends repeating the name, she simply said, "The cat." Drake stood by her side and peered out.

"You brought Nepeta cataria! Use it, girl!" He cried. Feeling incredibly stupid, Nyx looked at him. He winked at her and patted her on her head. "First thing you need to do, is to relax. Let's have some tea then we can put our heads together. Maybe have a little sleep, too." He yawned. It was contagious. Alva let out a long yawn. She made up three makeshift beds out of Chamomile leaves. "Between the tea and the leaves, we'll have a grand nap."

Nyx woke with a start. She heard what sounded like sniffling. She peered out from under the leaves. Nothing. She could hear deep breathing on either side of her. Quietly, she pushed the leaves off of her and got up and stretched. Again, the odd sound filled the space. She stopped and listened again, but this time, she saw a shadow go across the floor outside the baseboard. Instantly she knew: Hitch. She tried to see, but the house was dark, too. She moved away from the tiny opening and went to the shelf Alva made. She opened her wings and lit them. The room glowed in a warm yellow light. She scanned the shelf until she found the Nepeta cataria, or as the Humans called it, catnip. She didn't realize it could help her almost as much at it would help the Human. Catnip was used by Fae because it's beneficial as a medicinal tea to abate coughing, relieve cold symptoms and upset stomach, and to assist sleep. Who knew it would play a major role in helping her stay alive! She gathered a sprig and quickly removed the leaves. She gathered four more sprigs. Working quickly, she turned the leaves into a fine powder. She put this into a satchel and, holding it tightly, went to the opening. She slowly peered out, looking for anything white. She saw nothing. Carefully squeezing her body and the satchel through, she let out a breath. She waited. All was quiet. She opened her wings, and illuminated them. Not fully; she only needed a guiding light. Just enough so that she would not fly into anything. The first task, to find Hitch and give him something to keep him occupied with anything but a flying pixie.

14

She found him exactly where she thought he'd be. On the Human's bed, sleeping. For now, the catnip could wait. She then flew gently (so the buzzing and the breeze from her wings would not startle Hitch awake) to the head of the bed. The covers were a mess. She could not see the Human. Turning, she looked at Hitch. Still sleeping. She then flew to the pillow and cautiously landed. She slid down it. It almost made her giggle. *"That was fun!"* she thought. Back to business. She looked under the sheet. No Human. She looked around and tried to climb back up to the top of the pillow, but it was way too slippery! She would have to grab onto the pillowcase and that might wake up the damned cat.

She jumped off of the bed and took off. She flew out the door and landed on the threshold. She knew she had just seriously put herself in grave danger. If the Human had seen her, or she had flown into her; her heart was racing. Catching her breath, she calmed down. Walking along the baseboards, she went down the hall. The lights from outside lit it up quite nicely. She came to the corner and stopped. She could see most of the couch from where she stood. Nothing. No Human. She looked to the right. A rocking chair. Empty. She ran across to the other wall. Again she looked around the living room. No Human.

Around the corner was a bathroom. She would have to walk (or fly) around the corner in order to see the bathroom door. Taking a deep breath, she ran. She slid on the polished wood floor, and crashed into the wall across from the bathroom and slammed against the wall. A bookshelf stopped her from gliding across the floor. Rubbing her head, she let her legs splay out in front of her. She felt lost all over again. In her mind, she retraced her steps and finally figured out where she was. The bathroom was just beyond the bookshelf, on the left. She stood up and again, rubbing her head, she quickly walked in front of the bookshelf until it ended. She rested there for a moment then ran to the wall. She walked with her back to it, using her tiny hands to feel where she was going. It was dark here. Her hands felt a change in the wall and she knew it was the opening to the bathroom. The trim was slick, and her sweaty hand nearly made her slip. Wiping her hands onto her knees, she turned and, holding onto the molding, she saw that the door was open and no one was inside. Empty.

She walked inside. Only a sink and a toilet in here. No shower. A fear now began to grow inside her belly. Fear also fed an even bigger need to find the Human. Forgetting herself, she flew out the door, down the hall back to the living room. She hovered there, looking around. A sudden flash from outside startled her. Then, explosive thunder made her fall. Within seconds, Alva and Drake were hovering beside her.

"What the hell are you doing, Girl? Get back to the shelter! Are you crazy!?" He whispered to her. "This is not how you do this! You're going to ruin this if you don't start using your head!" Alva was whimpering.

"He's right, Nyxie. Please come back with us! It's not safe! You can't just fly around a Human's house!" Nyx was too worried and scared to listen. She broke free from them and flew into the kitchen. She looked around, wildly. With each passing second, her hopes for finding her Human safe were dwindling. Thunder blasted again. Alva and Drake found her standing on top of the kitchen curtains. They flew up and joined her, distinguishing their lit wings. They found her sobbing.

"I can't find her. She's not here! Oh, Drake, where is she?" He hugged her close.

"Nyx, this house still has another floor. I must insist that you come back to the shelter now. We can search together in the morning, the correct way. Why did you do this? You haven't any idea on how to deal with Humans! You can't just go out and look for them like that! There is too much risk involved. So much can go wrong! Now, come with us and we will tell you what to do. We will sleep and then, with a clear mind, we will begin. Actually, we shall start right now. We will walk back. Walk, not fly."

"I know, I know!" As much as she loved him, sometimes she just wanted to punch him in the mouth.

Nyx lay in her makeshift bed. Tears rolled off a cheek. She felt like a child being punished. Still, she knew that Drake was right. There was still so much she didn't know about the Humans. There were things that must be avoided. The line between Fae and Humans was strong but at the same time it was incredibly fragile.

Approaching this without skill and precision could result in disastrous outcomes. Her world could be forever changed; not just hers, but the entire Fae world as well. The Human world was simply not ready to accept the Fae world, and until it could, certain protocols must be followed.

Most Fae do not trust the Humans. They are very wary of them, even taking steps to avoid them. While the fascination with them is always there (think of how Humans are fascinated with Fae), most Fae are very devout to Mother Earth, and watching Humans disrespect it angers them greatly. Fae will occasionally stumble into a Human's garden. Seeing a well-tended garden will always earn a Faerie's respect. Even more rarely, a Fae may hear a Human's prayer. Some Humans seek Fae. They will fashion their gardens with sweet little nooks and hiding places for them. Some leave little treats for them, hoping the squirrels won't find them first. These are the Humans Fae seek out. Some Humans attract Fae without even trying to. If a home is kept neat and tidy, and lovely plants and flowers are around, and an obvious love and respect for Mother Earth is noted, Fae will want to be around them. If only Humans could accept them without destroying the delicate line that separates them.

Nyx often thought about how the two worlds would live if Fae were discovered. Most Fae liked not being noticed. They liked their tiny world, green, lush and plentiful. War was something Fae could not grasp. Sure, they can disagree, but to kill another over something? It was unheard of. To see the Humans kill each other. And some Humans killed when not at war! Why? Fae just didn't understand, and this fear kept them out of the Human world. That's not to say all Fae are sweet and sparkly. Some were downright disgusting and hateful. Still, killing was just not in their blood. They had other ways of hurting and belittling.

Her thoughts returned to Lila. She knew in her heart that she was very ill now. Something she could not pinpoint was telling her. She would let her friends teach her things she needed to learn in order to find out for sure if she was okay. She didn't know this Human, but something told her she must get to know her. She felt Lila had a sadness to her. She didn't know why, but the longer she stayed in this house, the stronger she felt about Lila. But what to do about it?

15

Lila got out of the shower and toweled herself dry. The hot shower felt so good. There is something about showering after you leave a hospital; all of the horrible smells and the stickiness. It was disgusting. She scrubbed hard using Ivory soap. Knowing how much that dried her skin out, she then used her favorite shower gel on her purple pouf. Hearing the water gurgle down the drain, it felt as if all the ugliness of the hospital drained away as well.

She put on some light green velour pajamas. Where she left the house feeling very cold, now she was burning up and sweaty. Still, she knew drafts were her enemy and she dressed warmly. She reached behind her and opened the window. Just a crack.

Erin brought her home and made sure she was okay before leaving to go fill her prescriptions, but before she left she put the soup back onto the stove and slowly it came to the boil. Lila was still very sick and needed to rest, but she felt she would be okay by herself. Erin returned and brought Lila the huge antibiotic pills she needed, plus a stack of trashy tabloid magazines. She made sure Lila ate and then offered to sleep over. Lila thanked her but told her she'd be okay alone. When Erin protested, she smiled, thanked her again, and shooed her home.

The soup was amazing. It felt so good on her now raw throat. Putting her mug onto the table, she grabbed her cell and called Roan.

"You sound better. How do you feel?" he asked. "Where are you?"

"I'm home. I feel like crap. I hurt everywhere. I took off the rest of the week. If I get fired, at least I'll get unemployment. Screw 'em. I miss you." She had to stop talking. A tickle was starting at the back of her throat. She knew a fit was beginning.

"Oh, Lila. I miss you, too. Why isn't Erin there? I thought she was going to stay with you? You shouldn't be all alone." Hearing Lila coughing, he continued. "Oh damn. I'm sorry. You should stop talking. I'll talk. Okay? " Lila cleared her throat.

"Okay."

"Let's see; the funeral is set for this Saturday. At two. Our Lady of Lourdes on Sean McDermott Street in Dublin. Burial will be at Huguenot Cemetery in Merrion Row. It's beautiful there, Lila. Bluebells are all over the place. I wish you could see them! "He said wistfully. He continued. "I will be leaving first thing Sunday morning. I will fly into London, then straight into Portland International. I'll just cab it straight to you. I just want to get this week over with and come home to you. I'm never leaving you again, Lila. Let's get this wedding of ours planned! Okay?" Lila, as sick as she was, felt giddy. She couldn't wait for him to come.

"Roan, I don't care about wedding plans anymore. I just want to marry you. I don't need a big church, or a crazy white gown, or flowers or cake; I don't give a shit. I just want to be your wife. I'd gladly and proudly marry you if you showed up in a potato sack." She started coughing, again. "Just come home to me, safely, Roan." He promised her he'd do just that. She hung up feeling happier than ever. Still, she felt herself shiver and knew her temperature was rising again. She took her glass and mug to the sink. She got a glass of fresh water and took some Tylenol. Now all she wanted was her soft, warm bed.

16

"We never travel alone. We travel and frolic in troops." Drake eyed Nyx sternly. Nyx eyed him back just as much. They quickly found their way back to the shelter where Alva waited. Food was forgotten and they needed to eat, soon. Together they carried a huge oak leaf that held gooseberries, tiny blueberries and a few tubers. Nyx nearly tripped on a twig, causing her to lose her grip on her end of the leaf. Berries and tubers fell at her feet. She wanted to scream, but instead took a deep breath and addressed Drake.

"Look. I am an adult. Don't talk to me like I'm some feeble child. I know our ways. I know we never travel alone. Yes, I did it. Get over it. Just tell me what I need to do so that I can approach this Human, okay?" she said angrily as she slammed their food onto the leaf. "I'm not a child!" she yelled. She was hushed by Alva at the entrance. Drake spun around,

"Then stop acting like one. Sometimes you act like a spoiled kid."

"Please stop yelling. You'll wake her!" Alva whispered. "She's asleep. At least, I think she is. I hope she is." She shook her head worriedly. Nyx, together with Drake, put the leaf onto the musty floor.

"She's here? You saw her?" Nyx ran to Alva, grasping her shoulders. "How do you know?" Nyx grinned. She then ran to the edge of the baseboard and peered out. Drake pulled her back inside.

"This is exactly what I mean. You don't know when stop, do you? Nyx, please watch what you're doing!" Drake's voice was a low growl. "Now. Alva. What did you hear?" He looked at her, expecting an answer.

"I need music. We forgot the instruments. We must have music!" Alva paced, nervous and distracted. Seeing the looks on both of her friends' faces, she relaxed. "I'm sorry. I heard them come inside. Keys. Voices. It sounded like there were two of them. Two female Humans, women! Two women. One was a bit older than the other, the sick one. Oh, she sounds terrible. Coughing up a storm. It's terrible." Alva's lip began to tremble.

Nyx approached her again. "Don't cry! Don't cry. Tell me. Is this older – woman – is she still here?" Alva sat on a flat nail head, eating a blueberry. She'd forgotten just how hungry she was. Alva took one as well and sat in front of her. Sniffling, Alva took a bite of her berry and said,

"No. She made food for her and then went home. The sick one ate, and then spoke to someone. She sounded sad, then so happy." Drake drank some honeysuckle nectar, belched then added,

"I bet it's a man!" he said in a sing-songy voice. "Whoopee! She has a lover! She's in love!" Alva grinned.

"She was told to take medicine to bring the fever down. Bad medicine. We need to make our potion. It'll work. Better than that awful pill. We could brew her a tea-potion." Drake swallowed.

"All in good time." Drake said, mouth full of blueberry. Nyx stood.

"But that's just it. She's sick now. Alva is right; she needs a tea-potion. We can do this. Drake? Please. We can also clean up her kitchen. Put the soup away and make her sink shine!" Drake considered this.

"Yes. We can do this. But, only if you listen to me. Pay attention to my directions. I also think flowers from her garden would look nice in the living room. Let's eat a decent supper then we will get to work." Nyx flew up and did a somersault. She lit her wings, sparkling a bright teal blue, and flew into a heart formation. Green shimmering dust slowly fell into a heart and disappeared. Drake smiled, shaking his head.

"Yes, my friend; I love you too."

***

Picking flowers in the dark was an interesting task in the Human world. Lots of creatures were out at night. Some might enjoy a little Pixie for an appetizer. They worked quickly, hiding from the occasional set of red eyes in the bushes. Raccoons and mice. Nyx had the three of them tidy the Human's porch. They could not fly outside here, especially at night. Sure, they might blend in with the fireflies, but still, it was a big risk. Plus, Drake's garish wings would always glow a deep magenta, making him an even greater risk. They gathered blossoms and took them back around to the portal by a willow tree in the backyard. Passing the hard, musty roots, they found the familiar soft earth and walked quickly to the light of the baseboard. The kitchen light had been left on and it acted as a beacon showing them the way.

As soon as they were back in the shelter, they unloaded more flowers and nectars, berries and tubers. Nyx took to the shelf and removed the catnip. Adding cinnamon and chamomile, she crushed them into a woody mess. Drake was busy trying to build a fire.

"Won't the Human smell the smoke?" Nyx asked him.

"No, unless it burns for too long. I need to bring this nectar just to the boil then I'll extinguish it. Bring me the crushed herbs." Soon a potion was steeping and the fire was out. "All we need is to make sure a few drops of our tea-potion with her tea." Nyx listened intently as she knew the next part was the real exciting part. "Then we must take it to her kitchen. She is still asleep so it will be easy. Together, and only together, we will fly; I will carry the potion. I have a flask. I will need help with the water. We need to boil at least a cup of water. We will find something to use. If we work together, we can do this. I may have to make a few trips to her bedside table to fill a teacup. We need to find one." Drake's voice faltered. "We may have to spend tonight just gathering what we need. A teacup. It can be a small one. If she has one, at all." He scratched his back, in thought. Alva spoke, worried as usual,

"That will never work, Drake. Let's look for a cup now. We will just have to make sure that the tea is placed here. We can time it for when morning comes. The good thing about this potion is that it tastes wonderful, hot or cold. I think that's the only way, Drake." She drummed her long fingers on the counter.

"Yes. I agree. Sometimes, you truly surprise me, kiddo. Come on. Let's get to work!" he said with a raised eyebrow. Alva blushed.

"We could have used magic. This was hard, Drake!" Nyx said, her breath coming in fast puffs. "Why do this the hard way?" Drake too was out of breath. Fanning himself with a torn honeysuckle leaf, he replied,

"Of course we could have used magic, dear. And eventually that is all you will use, but until you fully understand how badly things can go wrong, especially with that damned cat roaming around, we'll save magic for later." Looking at Nyx, he understood her. "Look, I know you're anxious. I'm anxious. Girl, I have clothes to make. I have threads to spindle! And I know the Human is ill. I think we can start using magic tonight. Let's see how the tea goes. Then, we'll set forth. There are still a few very important lessons I think you need to learn, but I promise to be straight-forward about them. No more surprises. Deal, kiddo?" Nyx smiled. "Ah! I know you're happier; you're teal is showing!" Nyx had a lovely glow surrounding her tiny body.

"I am so grateful to you. To the both of you!" She hugged Drake tightly. She then turned and kissed Alva on the cheek. Seeing Alva's worried eyes, Nyx tousled her silver hair.

"It'll be fine, Alva. Wait and see." Alva swallowed. Blinking her weepy yes, her body suddenly straightened." Come on, stop being a downer! The fun is about to begin!" Nyx laughed as she stood and pulled Alva up to stand in front of her. Alva nodded.

"You're right! Enough tears. We can do this. I can do this. No more tears. Promise!" Alva proclaimed proudly. Drake engulfed the two in his long arms, hugging them close.

"We are Pinkies, loners. We always will be. But together, we are a strong force. Each of us has a uniqueness; each of us has our own powers. That, in and of itself, is amazing. Put us together and we are just about invincible. We live until we are killed by another. But remember, when we die, we are then reborn, but only if we have lived a good and happy life." He kissed his friends, each on a cheek. He motioned for them to sit before him. He leaned against a broken board. He spoke again, his voice deep and reverberating. "Faeries are born designed to help people, Humans. It takes a while to realize and understand this. Years. Just like you, Nyxie. We begin to realize that we don't feel right if we aren't helping them. If a Faerie lives many lives, and has too much pressure, despair, and stress that they can't situate," He looked at Alva and nodded, "they will sometimes snap and become little more than vegetables. When this happens, their Mother Faerie knows instantly and calls them back. She takes care of the Faerie until it is their time to die again, and then catches the Faerie soul before it can Reincarnate. She will release the soul into the world, and it will no longer Reincarnate."

Alva frowned. Drake knelt down in front of her, taking her tiny hand.

"Some say magic is really Souls of Faeries who have gone through this but were able to save themselves. I believe that; Faeries are always meant to help. We will only be at peace if we know we are helping someone, a Human." Nyx sighed and said,

"So you do understand my heart. This is how I have felt for the past few days. I always knew I would someday feel this way, I just never knew when. Or what would finally lead me to it. I have finally found it. Why did it take me so long to feel such an urgency to help this Human, this person?" Drake popped a blueberry into his mouth. Nodding as he chewed, he spoke.

"Like I said, we are born this way. Something in our past is blocking us from fully feeling it. We – Alva and I – are the unlucky ones. We have never found it. Only you. And yet it took you this long to truly feel it in your soul. Alva and I have a great desire to help you on your journey. You are destined to live with this Human! Just seeing your concern for her now is a great sign that this is your destiny, Nyxie. It is up to you how you want to proceed. It is up to me to guide you. The three of us were born miles apart, but we were born with a ring of friendship bound tightly around us. In the proper moment, we were brought together, for life. No matter where we live, now we will always be bound."

17

A coughing fit gripped Lila so fiercely she felt as if her ribs were going to snap. She braced herself, holding onto a dining room chair. She took a deep breath and winced. It hurt to breathe. She exhaled and slowly took in another breath. It was easier this time. Satisfied that her fit was over, she walked into the kitchen. She needed to keep drinking. She was exhausted though and the thought of having to make a simple cup of tea only made her feel worse, like it was hard work. Taking a glass out of the cupboard, she filled it a quarter of the way with water. She drank it down and grimaced. Placing the glass into the sink, she noticed how shiny it was. Funny, she didn't remember Erin cleaning up before she left. She probably had. *Thank God for Erin*, she thought, making a mental note to get her a little something nice to thank her later.

She went into the bathroom and looked into the mirror. Sticking out her tongue, she looked at herself. She shivered and looked at her teeth. "I'll brush them later," she said to her reflection. Her head was pounding again. She flipped off the light and headed back to the kitchen. She knew staying hydrated was very important right now, and no matter how bad she felt, she had to drink. Stifling another cough, she went to the cupboard by the pantry and got out the kettle and some tea. As she brought the kettle to the sink, she turned on the water to fill it. It was then that she again and noted just how clean and sparkly her sink was and that the glass she had just used was gone. She filled the kettle, frowning. Switching off the water, she set the full kettle onto the counter and looked behind her. The glass wasn't on the kitchen table. She returned to the sink and looked on the counters surrounding it. Nothing.

I'm losing my mind. I know that glass was here.

She put the kettle onto the stove and turned on the gas. She opened the cupboard to get a cup and saucer. She noticed then that the glass was now sitting right next to the cup and saucer. Clean and dry. A coldness swept over her body. Her hair stood on end, this time not from fever but from fear.

What? I know I put that glass in the sink.

She looked out her kitchen window. She saw nobody. It was still early, but light enough to see. Erin's car was still in the driveway. She pulled the sheers apart and looked. Suddenly she heard a door slam and then saw Erin rushing to her car; fumbling with her keys. She glanced Lila's way. She smiled.

"I'll call you when I get to the office!" she yelled. Lila heard her and nodded uneasily. Erin nodded quickly and got into her car and drove away. She let the curtains close. Feeling her unease rising, she pulled a chair out in the dining room. She sat with a hard *Thump!* and looked around her dining room. Her eyes were then averted to the right as she saw Hitch coming into the living room and watched him stretch. Soon he was purring around her leg and mewing loudly.

"Okay. Let's get you fed." She went back to the pantry and found the tin of cat food. Hitch meowed louder. "Settle down, hungry boy, it's coming." Her insecurities were easing, but she still sensed something just wasn't right as she opened the tin. She set Hitch's bowl down and washed her hands, scrunching up her nose. As sick as she was, the pungent odor of cat food made her cringe. "Disgusting." She shook her head, fighting the urge to gag. The kettle began its screaming and Lila put a teabag into her cup. She then poured the water and carefully dunked her bag. She took the cup and saucer to her bedroom. She knew the tea was boiling hot, so by the time she could shower, it would be perfectly steeped and a bit cooler.

***

"Go. Now!" Drake loudly whispered to Nyx as he pushed her toward the opening at the baseboard. "She's showering. Go. I'll be watching!"

***

The hot water felt so good. So did a good shampooing. Lila rinsed and put on a bit of conditioner to work while she shaved her legs and armpits. She let the steam enter her lungs. Taking another deep breath, she was wracked with pain and another fit of agonizing coughing. She rinsed her hair just enough to get the gooey lather out and stepped out of the tub. Instantly, she was overcome by cold and she shivered intensely. She would have stepped right back in and showered more, but the hot water was now gone. She decided that this was the absolute worst she had felt in all of her life. She put her robe on while she was still dripping wet and pulled a thick towel off the rack and covered her wet hair tightly. Her teeth hurt because she was shivering so intensely.

The mere thought of walking made her shiver more. *The breeze will kill me*. She thought. *So cold*. She knew her tea was now ice cold and she actually started crying. She felt so sick and alone. She needed Roan here with her. "Roan! I need you here...please, come home. Please," she cried. Crying made her head and chest burn. She ripped off some toilet paper and wiped her nose. Her head spun. Infection poured out into the tissue. Seeing this made her instantly turn and vomit onto the floor. "Oh, God. Kill me," she sobbed.

Her entire body was engulfed in pain. Even her hair hurt. *Bed. Just get to the bed, Lila*, she encouraged herself. *You can clean later. S-so cold*. Violent chills overcame her. She slid into the bed, pulling on anything that would cover her and curled into a shivering ball. Her wet hair hung in soggy ribbons across her face. She didn't care. *I don't want to die; please God. Bring Roan to me. Don't let me die*. Her eyes closed. She felt Hitch jump onto the bed. He plopped his fat body down against her back and began purring. "Keep me warm, Hitchie," She mumbled and soon fell into a deep sleep.

18

"Good job, but now you'll have to do it all over again. She's asleep. Don't let that give you a false sense of security, though. You'll have to work quickly and silently. You can do this!" Drake reassured her.

***

Lila was awakened by the sound of her cell phone ringing. She almost cried. She had finally found the perfect position and was perfectly warm. The thought of poking her arm out of the blankets sent her into another fit of chills. Ignoring the phone, she tucked her knees as close to her chin as she could and ducked her head beneath her comforter. Whoever it was would simply have to wait. Thankfully, Lila fell right back to sleep.

What seemed like minutes later, but was actually four hours later, the phone rang again. This times Lila's body was soaking wet. Her pajamas were stuck to her now slick body. Throwing off the covers she reached for her phone.

"I tried calling you two hours ago. I guess you went back to bed?" Erin's worried voice had a tinge of annoyance to it. Clearing her throat, Lila croaked into the phone.

"Yeah, I did. Sorry. I just..." She began coughing. Hard coughs that made every nerve in her body scream. "Oh, God this sucks." Her hair was still wet. It had never dried and she could not tell whether it was because it was from showering or because she was sweating so much. Her back and ribs ached. "I'm going to take another shower and then warm up some soup." Lying back down, she held the phone to her ears, squeezing her eyes shut. She pinched the corners of her eyes hard, wincing.

"Do you need anything? I could come by and..." Lila cut her off by coughing.

"No, really. I'm fine," she said as Erin laughed.

"Yeah, Doll, you sound like you are. Look, call me if you need anything. I'll be home around seven or so."

Lila thanked her and clicked "end".' She sat up slowly. She really was soaked and it felt gross. Taking off the wet clothes, she crumpled them up into a ball and threw them across the room. She stretched. She slid to the side of the bed, and smelled something. It was a wonderful aroma, something she could not quite put her finger on. She looked around and finally looked at her nightstand. There was her tea cup.

It was steaming hot.

She squinted and looked closer. Yes, that was definitely steam. She frowned. *I made that tea hours ago. It should be ice cold. Should be.* Without thinking, she put her thumb and middle finger around the cup. She recoiled, nearly tipping it over. It was not just warm, it was hot. Hot enough to make her recoil.

"I'm losing my fucking mind!" A cold layer of fear poured over her body and she stood up. "What the hell is happening! Who is here!? WHO ARE YOU?"

***

"Okay, she knows something is up. Now is the time. Make yourself known to her. Be careful. Ease your way to her. No matter how gentle you are, you *will* scare her at first. She may even faint. Be yourself. If you need us, we can help you. It is best if you do this on your own, though." Nyx was nervously biting her nail.

"So what if you and Alva are seen by her? Can't that happen?" Alva was crying. "Will you stop that? Stop crying!" Nyx yelled. Alva's face twisted and she flew up high into the rafters, tears and pixie dust falling to the dirty floor under her. "Oh, dammit. Alva! Come back! I'm sorry!" she yelled, exasperated. Drake came to her.

"Don't worry about her. She'll be okay. We'll discuss this later, but you mustn't wait any longer, you have to present yourself to the Human, now! Go!" Drake then pulled her arm. He kissed her cheek and smiled at her. "This is what you have been waiting for all of your life. Now go." He smiled at her and nodded toward the baseboard. Nyx took a deep breath and flew out the opening.

She could hear the Human yelling. She landed just outside the bedroom door and peered inside. The Human was removing her panties and then ran out the door, right past her to the shower. She saw the door slam and the water turn on. *She's panicking*, Nyx thought. Without hesitation, Nyx flew over to the messed-up bed. Moving with a flash of light, she removed the soiled bedclothes. She waved her hands and in an instant the bed was made. Then she flew toward the closet and picked up the soiled clothes and underpants. Waving her hands again, in a flash of light, they were clean and folded. She set them at the end of the pristine bed. She then flew to the nightstand. She waved her arms and in a last bright green flash, cleaned the spilled tea and a brand new steaming fresh cup appeared.

Hearing the water stop, she flew up to the top of the lacy canopy and lay down. She flipped her tiny body over and lay on her stomach, inching her way toward the edge of the fabric of the canopy. It was lacy and she could slip through the holes if she was not careful. She grabbed the edge and looked over. She saw the Human. Wet and coughing. She looked terrified. As soon as the Human entered the room, she saw the bed with its clean bedclothes newly laid out pajamas and she screamed.

"Oh my God! What the fuck is happening? Who is here!? I'm calling the police. I have a gun and I'll use it! I'll fucking kill you!" A fit of coughing hit Lila so hard it brought her to her knees. She saw the pajamas and panties. Standing up, she picked them up. "What are you doing!? Get out of my house!" She threw the pajamas onto the floor. Again, she started coughing. It was then that she saw the tea, still hot and steaming. "I don't know what the hell you want from me, but please just go away. Please?" She sniffled, kneeling to the floor. She dropped her head into her hands. It was then that she heard the tiny voice,

"The tea will cure you. I promise."

Lila lifted her head and gasped. Hot pain seared through her skull, but so did a fear she'd never felt before; it tore through her chest.

"Oh, please. Oh, please. Oh, please go away," she whispered, looking around. The voice was so tiny that she could not determine where it was coming from. She was now trembling so hard she had to brace herself against her dresser. She realized that she was naked and fumbled with the drawers for clothing. She didn't even look to see what she was putting on. "I mean it. I – I have a gun," She lied. She looked around the room again. She listened. She stood at the foot of the bed and looked at it closely. It was beautifully made. Even the sheets were tucked in. She walked slowly around toward the nightstand. The tea was steaming. She could not wrap her mind around any of it. If someone was there to rape or rob her, would they wash her clothes, wash and replace her bed linens, and make not one, but two cups of tea for her? She reached for her cell phone. "I'm calling the police, now!" she yelled. Suddenly, a soft voice said,

"Please don't. I'm only trying to help you. I mean you no harm! I – I'm scared too." Lila dropped her cell phone. She squeezed her eyes closed tightly and bit her lip

"Please," the little voice continued, "I know you are very ill. I am here to help you. I want to be your friend." Lila's eyes popped open. She looked at the floor, afraid to look anywhere else. The tiny voice seemed to come from behind her.

"Who are you? Why are you doing this?" Lila suddenly spun around. She looked at the bed. Nobody was there. "Where are you!" Lila lost her balance. Her head pounded and she began coughing fiercely. She felt the beginnings of another fever building. She leaned on the edge of the bed to keep from falling.

"Up here," the little voice said. Lila slowly stood up. She turned around and her head tilted up. At first she saw nothing. Moving closer, she could see two tiny hands. They were holding on to the edge of the canopy. Her mouth opened. She shook her head. Was she seeing things? The tiny fingers moved. They gripped the edge tighter.

"What are you? Who," Suddenly the doorbell rang. Lila jumped. She saw the tiny hands let the canopy go. There was a flash of light, and then nothing. Lila pulled the fabric of the canopy down with her index finger; gone. Whatever it was, it was gone. Seeing nothing, she then stepped on the edge of her bed and looked on top of the canopy. Nothing. The doorbell rang again, followed by an annoying rapping. She sneered at the interruption, instead of welcoming what could be help. She jumped down and ran to the door. Running instantly made her start coughing. She opened the door. Erin's smile quickly turned into a frown.

"Oh, my God. You look like shit, Lila. Your face is all red, and ... you're naked! For Chrissakes, come sit down before you cough up a lung!" Lila let Erin guide her to the couch. Erin ran into the bedroom and found her bathrobe. She brought it to Lila. She sat and looked at Erin. Lila was honestly at a loss for words. Erin walked into the kitchen and filled a glass with water. "Drink it." Lila took the glass and eagerly gulped the entire glassful in three long swallows. "Thirsty, huh? How are you?" Erin sat in the rocking chair, looking like she was going to be staying a while. Lila simply looked at her. "Hello?" Erin waved her hand. Lila's eyes slowly focused on Erin's. "Damn, girl. Just what kind of drugs did they prescribe for you? Hello!" Lila shifted nervously on the couch. She looked around the room, trying to gather words.

"I – I'm doing better. I'm just really sore from coughing and I'm, I'm very tired still. I – I took the rest of the week off." Her teeth began chattering uncontrollably. "Look, I would love to sit and chat," Erin nodded.

"I know. Get yourself to bed. You seem to be doing okay. I won't call anymore if you promise to call me tomorrow. Tomorrow, okay?" Lila nodded and smiled. "If I don't hear from you, I'm coming over. I mean it." Lila got up and forced a smile, nodding.

"Promise. Thank you. Now, go before I infect you." She closed the door and locked it. She watched Erin turn the corner to her sidewalk. She shivered and slowly walked to her bedroom. The room was now bright with sunlight. The blinds were opened. On the bed, fresh pajamas lay out neatly with fresh cotton panties on top of the pajama bottoms. Lila approached the bed. She slowly sat on the mattress, running her hand along the pajamas. She suddenly heard a strange sound. Like a humming-bird, or a bumble bee flying right by her ear. The noise startled her and she instinctively spun around, away from the sound. She tried to follow the sound. Slowly, she looked up. The two tiny hands slowly grasped the edge of the lacy canopy again. Looking closely at them, she noticed that they had a slight bluish-green tint to them. She was scared, but also intrigued.

Curiosity was quickly overshadowing fear. Her courage mounting, she stepped on the bedrail and grabbed onto the bed post, hoisting herself up. She saw the tips of what looked to be four wings appear. Then she saw the hair, a silky black-blue. She swallowed hard. She felt a cough coming on and turned her head away from the tiny body. She swallowed hard, determined not to let the itch in her throat win. Satisfied that she would not cough, she looked back at the strange being. She slowly inched closer and finally saw a tiny perfect little face. It looked just as scared as she felt. She heard the being gasp and saw it cover its mouth to stifle a scream. When the creature moved, Lila gasped. Still, the two beings stared at each other for what seemed like minutes. Lila was too shocked, too amazed to move. The tiny being slowly let her hand fall away from her mouth. Licking her tiny lips, the creature forced a smile.

"H-hello." Lila herself stifled a scream. "Don't be afraid!" The pixie asked quickly, but so softly. Lila's mouth stayed open. "I know this seems really strange," the creature said. Seeing the look on the Human's face, she relaxed. The creature's eyes, big and green, sparkled. Suddenly, the creature's face changed and she giggled. "You should see your face!" The look on the Human's face changed to total disbelief. This made the tiny creature laugh hysterically. Her little head fell forward, her face bouncing into the lacy fabric as she laughed. Soon she rose up, resting her pointy chin on her palms, elbows sinking into the canopy. She turned her head sideways and smiled at the Human. "Did you ever think you would ever have a conversation with a real pixie? I never thought I'd have one with a *real* Human! Honestly, is this insane or what?" The pixie rested her head on her arm, smiling up at Lila, her tiny feet twisting happily in the air.

"N-no. I – I never thought – where did – where are you from? And how did you ..." The pixie instantly sat up, crossing her legs, Indian-style.

"Before I tell you anything, let me say this: right now, I am here to help and protect you. Don't be afraid of me. You are very, very ill. I have tried to brew you three cups of tea. My tea will cure what ails you. All of those medicines you are taking, they will not cure you. My tea will. I promise it's safe. I would never do anything to harm you. That is against not only all Fae law, but Fae – um, faeries themselves – can become ill and die if they betray ever a Human. Faeries help people!" Nyx explained, shrugging. "We spend our lives looking for a person to attach to. Some never find that person and spend their entire lives searching until they are killed. Some Fae, they never find their Human-mate. I'm rambling, aren't I?" She giggled. Lila braced herself, still holding onto one of the bedposts. Her bare feet hurt digging into the bedframe.

"Are you telling me that you are a *faerie*? Like Thumbelina? Or Tinkerbelle?" she asked the creature, eyes unblinking. "Where is your magic wand? You've got to be kidding me. This fever is worse than I thought." she said, almost angrily. Suddenly there was a turquoise aura around the faerie's tiny body and she lifted with ease off of the canopy, her delicate wings spinning, her inky hair flowing. Lila sucked in a quick breath. She watched as the pixie rose and then darted across the bedroom, leaving green glittery specks of Fae dust behind her. Her tiny wings fluttered, shining in iridescences of purples, greens and blues, outlined in gold. She wore a white bodice which clung tightly to her perfectly proportioned breasts, like a second skin. A light blue blouse with airy sleeves. If she wore pants, Lila couldn't see them. Her hair, long and silky and blue-black, fell in soft, long rings. The faerie flew toward the Human and hovered near her shoulder. Lila stiffened, holding her breath.

"No magic wand," she said, opening her arms to prove she held no such object. "Sit. Please." Lila blinked then sat on the edge of her bed. "May I sit? I'm a bit winded." Lila only stared, nodding. "Thank you." The faerie landed on her knee. Lila felt nothing; the faerie's body was feather light. The creature's face changed again. A look of deep concern and a nod toward the steaming cup; "I beg you, please. Drink the tea. It's delicious, I promise! My own brew." She nodded proudly as Lila peered into the mist. "Anise, chamomile, and cinnamon. It will help to cure you, but you must drink it while it is steaming. That's part of the magic. Breathe in the steam. Go on." Lila frowned.

"You could be a wicked, evil faerie. Why should I trust you?" Lila could not believe not only what she had said, but that a faerie was in her house, engaging in intelligent conversation. "I am sitting in my bedroom, talking with a faerie. Slap me. Go on. Slap me!" she said in a half joking-half serious dare. The Fae looked at Lila, frowning.

"No. I never slap anyone." Lila looked at her, confused. The Fae continued. "I stumbled here by mistake a few days ago. I got lost, so lost! I was so scared! I found myself in your house, inside the walls. I saw how sick and sad you were. At first, all I wanted was to find my way out and go home. I did eventually find my way, but all of my thoughts returned to you. All I cared about was you," she confessed, her tiny booted feet dangling off of Lila's knee. "You are suffering, not only physically, but in your heart. Your lover is far from you. He aches for you as much as you ache for him. I cried for you for days. I knew you were my Human-mate at that very moment! You and I have been destined to be together since the day you were born, since the day I was born. It just took me this long to find you. If you let me, I can show you many things. You can show me many things. We are both unsure of each other's worlds. If you'll let me, I will be your protector. Protector of health and heart, spirit and love." She held her tiny hand out. Lila could not believe what she had just heard.

She found herself extending her huge hand, still very unsure of what was happening. Thinking the pixie would hold a finger, she jumped when the Fae leapt into her hand. "Bring me close to your face," The pixie whispered. Lila slowly raised her hand. The pixie caressed Lila's hot cheek. "Oh, dear. You're so feverish. Will you have me? I don't have to stay here. I know my way home now. Just so you know, I did set up a tiny area inside your wall. I had to study you. I must tell you that I belong to a tightly knit circle; two of my life-companions are in the wall right now. Drake is my mentor. He is teaching me what I need to know to ensure that my life with you is the best it can be. He is a water Fae. Alva is my best friend in the Fae world. Both of them are, actually. But they are both helping me, as they know of the Human world more than I. They will not stay after my training is completed. I can go, as well. My main priority is to first heal you, then get to know you and hope that you accept me. I will never interfere with your life. I just want to be here for you." A fat teardrop fell onto her wing. Lila felt her heart grow. She realized the how awesome yet so very delicate this moment was. He lip quivered.

"I hope you're for real. I hope I'm not in the middle of some really weird fever and drug-induced dream. I really want this to be real. Is this real? I don't even know what to call you. You must have a name?" Lila asked, sniffling. Shaking her wings dry, the pixie laughed.

"My name is Nyx. It means 'night.' I was born at night and my mother loved the night. Call me Nyxie, if you want. I like that. And you. You must have a name, too?"

"Lila." Nyxie beamed.

"Lila. Light! Your name means light. A beautiful name for a beautiful woman. You are the light in my darkness. See? We are destined to be together!" Lila let out a relieved laugh. "Now, before we talk further, please drink the tea. Change into the bedclothes I laid out, and then you can sleep. I will not leave your side. I'll feed that - that cat, too. Oh, and one more little thing. Until we talk more, I must insist that you tell no one about me. I will tell you why later, but it is imperative that my existence be kept a secret for now. Don't even tell your lover about me. Soon, but not yet. Promise me? My life, and the lives of my circle depend on that. Promise?" Lila smiled.

"Of course. I - yeah; I think that's a good idea. I don't think people would believe me, anyway. They might wanna lock me up in a nuthouse or something. Yes, I'll keep this our secret. The only other being that will know about you is Hitch." Nyxie frowned. "The cat."

"Ah! I have catnip for him. And for you. It's magical and very healing. Now, drink." She flew off of Lila's hand and stood next to the teacup. She watched as Lila drank. She sipped at first. A tiny sip. Nothing happened. Nothing bad, anyway. She sipped more. The hot liquid filled her mouth and soothed every nerve. While it did taste of cinnamon, chamomile and anise, there was also a flavor that was indescribable. It was so delicious. She felt her entire body relax, but not the way one would while taking drugs. This was a clean relaxation. A pure feeling of healing. She could feel the germs dying and her body strengthening. The heaviness in her chest began ebbing away. Nodding, Nyx added, "That's the catnip. Good stuff. Oh, and for future reference, don't ever try to brew catnip with the stuff you buy for Hitch. It'll pretty much kill you. I can do it. I prefer to use my herbs. I grow them at the brook by my holly bush. That's my home."

"You live in a tree? A holly bush? Do you ever stick yourself with the leaves?" Nyx flew to the edge of the bed and stood next to the pajamas.

"Put these on, you're all wet with fever. Yes! I hate that bush, I mean, I don't hate it; it's my home, but those thorny leaves could impale me! I could plant some of the herbs I use out in your backyard. Not only are they lovely, but it would be a lot easier to gather them and I wouldn't have to carry them on the day-long journey here from there. Well, we'll discuss more later. You must sleep now. I must report to Drake and Alva. I'm beat, too; it's been a day, hasn't it?" She asked, but didn't wait for Lila to respond. "Finish the tea and leave your cup there on the nightstand. I'll be checking on you. Get into bed now." Lila slid beneath the clean bedclothes. Nyx flew to her side on the pillow, her fragile wings fanning Lila. "Sweet dreams." She tentatively hovered low enough until she was just a hair away from Lila's cheek. She quickly kissed it. Lila smiled.

"Thank you, uh, Nyxie." Nyx smiled sweetly, then as quick as a blink, she rose and flew away. Lila pulled the covers close, turned onto her side, and watched the tiny faerie fly out of her bedroom. Her eyes shifted to the floor where they remained transfixed on the glittering emerald path Nyx left behind her.

19

"Come here, you minx! You were absolutely brilliant! Brilliant! I knew you could do it, Nyxie!" Drake hugged her tightly and swung her around in dizzying circles until they both fell to the floor, giddy. Alva ran to jump on top of them.

"You did it, Nyxie! I knew you'd do well! I knew it all along. What?" she asked as Nyx and Drake stopped laughing to give her their all too familiar "I told you so" stare. She grinned, sheepishly. They all laughed. "Seriously, I knew you would do it. I-I just ..." She suddenly began weeping. Drake rolled his eyes,

"Oh, good God, girl," he sighed, pushing them off of him. He brushed off his vest, shaking his head and glaring down at her. Alva tried not to cry, but failed. She ignored Drake and looked pleadingly at Nyx.

"I don't want to lose you, Nyxie. I love you like a sister. If you live here, what will we do?" Nyx leaned into Alva hugged her sobbing body close.

"You big silly. You'll never lose me. We are bound. Nothing can change that! Ever." She hugged her friend.

"You even remembered to tell her that this must remain a secret for a while. I'm very impressed." Drake added. Nyx nodded, releasing Alva.

"I think she wants to meet you two as well." Drake shrugged and replied,

"In time. Right now, you must concentrate on healing her. Once she is well, that is when you can truly get to know her. It's nice that she seems to like you so soon; she has most likely always been a believer in Fae. That's always a plus. Some Fae-Human homes are not friendly at all," he said, gathering fruits to prepare their meal. "The Humans know their Fae is around, and they accept it, for that is all some can tolerate. To actually see and talk to them might endanger them; some simply cannot handle it, Nyx. And that's fine. As long as there is an understanding, an unsaid contract if you will. They simply stay out of each other's way. For the most part, the Fae-Human relationship is a friendly one. This is what I want for you." Drake set a neatly decorated table of fruits, nuts, and of course, tea. "Come, let's eat! I'm starving."

***

Lila tried as long as she could to stay awake. Replaying the conversation over and over in her mind, she still thought it might be a crazy dream. Still, the glittery green dust was real. She dipped her finger into it and sure enough it stuck. She watched as it disappeared. And the tea! Three cups; steaming hot. And so delicious. Maybe it was her imagination, but she was starting to feel better. Still, she was very sleepy. *I've been drugged by a faerie*, were her last words before she drifted into a deep sleep.

She woke up hours later. The bedroom was now dark. She stretched and inhaled deeply. While it still hurt a bit, she definitely could breathe a lot easier. She instantly recognized the familiar aroma: tea. She looked at the night-stand and, sure enough, a steaming cup. She smiled. It was then that she saw a faint turquoise glow above the cup. It grew brighter, glittery sparkles of light glowed in the shape of four little wings.

"Hello! I imagine you slept well?" Nyx said with a smile. Lila stared with curious awe.

"Y-yes. Yes! I did. I feel," Lila watched as Nyx flew onto the bed, sitting on Lila's knee, "better. How..." But Nyx interrupted.

"That's my secret." Nyx nodded, knowingly. Seeing concern on Lila's face, she quickly added, "A safe secret. Remember, we do no harm. Drink up." Lila turned on the light and Nyx's eyes tightly squeezed closed. Her tiny hands shielding her eyes from the sudden bright intrusion.

"I'm sorry," Lila said, sadly. Nyx rubbed her eyes.

"No, no. It's fine! I'm not used to artificial light, that's all," she said, blinking. "It's kind of weird seeing light at this hour of the night!" Lila contemplated this as she sipped the glorious brew. Her eyes closed.

"This is so good." She savored the flavors. It also felt so good on her raw throat. Nyx suddenly left Lila's knee and flew way up.

"Good! Now get up and bring your tea into the bathroom. I've run a bath for you. Let's soak that ill out of you!" Lila only looked confused.

"But I just took a shower only..." Nyx interrupted.

"You did, but this is a healing bath. Come on, let's go!" Lila followed as Nyx flew ahead and darted sharply into the bathroom. An odd bluish glow poured of the room. Soon Lila could smell something different. Like a gentle pine or Rosemary scent. She saw that the room was dark but lit by candles, four of them. Three of them were blue. One was green. The room was warm and the bathtub was filled. The water looked milky, opalescent. It shimmered. Not glittery, but almost alive. The aroma and steam in the room were soothing. Lila put the teacup onto the little stool beside the tub. She smiled as she undressed. Nyx turned her head, respectfully. Sensing her unease, Lila smiled.

"It's okay. I don't mind if you see." Nyx giggled, facing the tiled wall.

"I know. We may be mates, but I will still respect your privacy." Lila nodded. "Now, get in. Tell me how it feels." Lila slid into her footed tub. Two things made her glad that she had this house: the kitchen and this bathroom. This was a huge tub, one of the old clawfoot bathtubs. A grown man could easily stretch out in it. It was deep, too. At first, the water seemed to be way too hot. She had to force herself into the water, but soon her body adjusted and she slid under it, letting out an audible sigh. Nyx turned and hovered above her. The milky water concealed Lila's body. "Well?" Lila smiled, closing her eyes. She took in another deep breath. The aroma was almost intoxicating.

"This is heavenly!" She said in ecstasy. "Wonderful. What is this? What am I smelling?" She ran her fingers through the water, watching the pearly currents swirl and change colors. Nyx flew to the toilet and with a deep breath, she blew air at the covered toilet seat lid. It fell with a loud *CLUNK*! Lila put her hand to her mouth and stifled a giggle. "I could have done that for you!" she murmured. Nyx landed on the fuzzy green cover and lay down on her tummy, resting her head on her hands. Breathing hard, she said,

"Next time, you shall." She caught her breath and then lifted her tiny body up to rest her chin on her palms. She lifted her legs behind her, kicking them happily, like a child. "Well, let's see, there's Essence of Opal. That's what makes the water look so cool. No real purpose, homeopathically. It's just really pretty!" she said with glee. "There's marjoram and pine needles. Ginger and mustard seed. And lavender. The marjoram will absorb infection, making it seep out of the pores, while the mustard seeds will absorb it." Lila suddenly looked horrified. Nyx looked at her, but nodded on. "The pine needles rejuvenate the skin. Ginger cleanses mucus membranes, and lavender does ... everything! While they all do their own jobs, mixed together, they are magic." Nyx's voice became a whisper. "When you get out of the tub, you will feel much worse, and your body will then purge out all of the infection and impurities that made you ill in the first place; you'll vomit. You will cough up terrible things and your nose and even your eyes will seep this viscous substance. That will only last an hour or so. The potion can only do so much." Seeing Lila frown, she flew to her. She sat on the tub's edge.

"But, then I'll be worse than I was before," Lila said fearfully. Nyx dipped her tiny foot into the water and kicked water at Lila. Tiny drops splashed Lila's face, making her scrunch her nose and blink. Droplets made rippling circles in the water, shimmering with rings of blue and purple.

"Of course you will! Silly minx! But I promise you, before midnight, you not only feel better, you will be *well,* again. Just wait and see! Now, relax and don't think about the bad. Think of the good. Close your eyes. Go on, that's it. Let the warm waters hug you," Lila closed her eyes. "Envision all of the poisons and toxins being pulled out of your body. Listen to my voice. See them. See them leave every organ. Every vein. Every capillary. Every cell. And finally every pore." Nyx's voice was like a soothing magnet, and Lila felt her entire being floating toward it; it pulled her, tickling her slightly. It surrounded her like a gentle, loving embrace. She could see the toxins leaving her. Nyx's voice slid through her. "Can you feel it? Try to feel the poisons exiting. They are." Suddenly, the stopper was removed from the drain, and the sound made Lila frown. "You will not be cold. Now, open your eyes, Lila. Envision the poisons and toxins flowing away, down the drain. All the things that made you feel so bad are now being released out of your body and they are flowing away." Nyx's voice sounded so far away now, its deep monotone surrounding her and reverberating in the room. "Stand." As she did, the shower turned on. Normally, that would have frightened her, but now it only made her grateful. She wasn't cold; the hot water hugged her like a soft blanket. "Rinse the toxins off of your body."

As she began, she noticed the nausea beginning. A look of horror spread across Lila's face. Nyx knew and commanded her: "Purge! Let it out!" Lila ran out of the tub and vomited violently into the toilet. "Let it out! Good, Lila, good!" Lila trembled. She felt her stomach squeezing and her body bent again as she retched. As she stood up, she saw her reflection in the mirror and it frightened her. Her eyes were beet-red and foul mucus was forming around them. This made her sick again, but only because it was just so disgusting and disturbing to see. She finally coughed and spat the last of the vile remains of the infection and stood.

"I need to finish. I need to shower," Lila said between breaths. Nyx nodded, agreeing.

"Shampoo your hair and now wash as you would normally. When you are done, dry off and meet me in the kitchen. You've done well, very well, Lila." Nyx flew up to Lila's slick shoulder. She stood there for a second, just long enough to kiss Lila's wet cheek and then, leaving a trail of green sparks, flew out the door.

20

Lila stretched out on the couch with Hitch curled up at her feet, purring in his sleep. She sipped broth that tasted very similar to beef consommé, but had a much milder flavor with hints of leek. It was delicious and warmed her to the bone. She listened to the wind outside. Putting her mug down, she reached for her cell phone and dialed Erin's number. Lila said she was feeling much better, and that she was thinking about going back to work tomorrow. After working on Friday, she'd still have the weekend to rest. She ended the call then quickly dialed Roan's number.

"It's so good to hear your voice! Can you hear me?" he yelled into the receiver. "Lila? Are you there?" Lila held the phone away from her ears, wincing.

"Geeze! Yes, I hear you! You don't have to yell. I hear you fine, sweetheart." She waited, smiling.

"Oh, okay. There," his voice returned to normal. "That better?"

"Much. You must be in town in if you have such a good connection." She shifted, waking Hitch. He yawned, stretching his long body, then jumped off of the sofa in search of food.

"Yes. I'm in a pub. It's quite nice. Quaint. Not crowded right now. There is a tower close by, and the reception is great here... and so is the food. I'm waiting for some colcannon. I miss that stuff!" His voice changed. "Tell me, how are you feeling? You sound better!" he said, swallowing his ale. "Sorry, you caught me mid-sip."

"I feel so much better. I don't know what's in those drugs, but they sure work fast!" She stifled a giggle. "I may even go back to work tomorrow. Not sure. I may work on my project for class. I really do feel a hell of a lot better." A sudden blast of lightening made her jump. "A storm is coming, I need to go. I just wanted to let you know that I was feeling better. I miss you so much."

"Can I call you later tonight? I would like to talk to you. I miss you, too. I love you. I'm so glad you're on the mend, kiddo. How about eleven? Can I call that late?" Lila's heart leapt.

"Of course. Okay. I'll talk to you then!" As she hung up, she saw a now familiar glow from around the corner near the hallway. "Hello, Nyx. Come sit with me." She sat up and set her phone on the coffee table. "Talk to me."

"Where's that cat. I don't want to be an appetizer," she asked, peering around nervously. Lila indicated that he was in the kitchen eating. Nyx leapt into the air and landed on Lila's knee.

"Comfy?" Lila asked. "Please, get comfortable." Nyx shifted on Lila's knee. "Okay. You knew this was coming; tell me about you," Lila said. Nyx blinked.

"What do you want to know?" Nyx asked, looking serious.

"Everything! Anything!" Lila said excitedly, making Nyx tumble off of her knee and get lost in the couch. Lila held out her hand and Nyx gratefully climbed into it. "I'm sorry! Here, sit here." Lila put a cushion onto her lap and gave it a gentle punch, making a perfect "chair" for Nyx, who flopped backwards into it. She wriggled her little body and finally snuggled in. She looked at Lila, again. Lila repeated, "Everything. Where are you from? Where to you live? Do you have parents? Are you married? Everything!" Lila smiled brightly. "I think I have a right to know, don't I? You know about me; us. Human beings. We know nothing about you, other than that nobody truly thinks you exist." Nyx nodded.

"True. You got me, there," Nyx said, scratching her leg." We do know about you - Human beings - because we have been taught to stay clear. That is, unless we find 'The One.' That'd be you. You're 'The One' for me. Before I found you, I feared Humans. Your world is so obviously bigger than mine, a perilous place. Not only do we risk exposure, we risk being killed. That is the only way Fae die, if we are killed by another Fae or a Human." Lila's eyes widened.

"You mean, you don't get sick? You don't get hurt?" Lila sipped more broth.

"Of course we get ill. We get hurt. Usually, we can heal ourselves. It's pretty rare for a faerie to die from illness. We can die from an injury, but only if that injury was intentionally given to kill. Does that make sense?" Lila turned onto her side and held her head in her hand, looking down at Nyx. She moved the pillow gently so she would not make Nyx fall. Lila shrugged.

"I guess so. So, you don't die from cancer, diabetes, or diseases like that?" Nyx nodded.

"That's right. See, Humans are very self-destructive. Not intentionally, at least that was the case thousands of years ago. You know so much more now and yet - there is so much you can do to stop disease," Nix said sadly. Lila's eyebrows knit into a frown.

"That's not fair. That's easier said than done. A person can try to be as healthy as possible by not drinking, or smoking, eating right, exercising. By not using pesticides when we grow our food and by not using harmful chemicals and still end up with cancer! Someone else is polluting the air with smoke, and exhaust. Factories belch all kinds of shit into the air." Lila sighed, "Anyway, we were talking about you - your world. So, what about - are you married? I guess Fae marry, don't they?" Nyx smiled.

"Some marry. Lila, Fae are very independent. Sure, we love. We have physical love, just like you do. I personally don't believe in marriage. I am not suited to be committed to just one person. I have many male friends. Some I love. If I were to ever find myself pregnant, I would certainly be thrilled and welcome a baby. But I don't believe that marriage is required for that. Most Fae agree with me. It's like we are all friends, the entire Fae world," She saw the look on Lila's face. "No, it's not a world-wide orgy. Matter of fact, sex is pretty sacred. It is not a casual thing, ever. Sexual relations between friends is not forbidden, but it is just not something we do. I have not found a person that I am content to share myself with, even at my age. I yearn for it. I dream about it. I too want a soul mate and I'm sure in time I'll find one. But I have other things I must focus on. Things that are more important. It will happen in time." Lila nodded and blinked.

"I love sex," she confided. Nyx 's hands immediately went straight to her mouth. Her already large eyes grew even bigger, and she giggled with a high-pitched glee that made Lila laugh. "It's true! I agree with you, though. It's special. I love Roan – my fiancé. He makes me feel beautiful. I hope you will want to meet him. Work. What about work? Do you have jobs?" Nyx got serious.

"Sure! We wander the earth and steal baby teeth from children." Lila almost spat her soup out. Stifling giggles of her own, she coughed and swallowed. Nyx still looked stern. "Sometimes, we build great chariots out of pumpkins so ugly stepsisters have a way to to go to the prom."

"You mean the ball." She was laughing heartily, now.

"Prom, ball, whatever." She could no longer keep a straight face and Nyx giggled again. She spoke after their laughter died down. "In all seriousness, no. We don't have 'jobs' like Humans do. We have responsibilities. We do these daily, no questions asked. It's a part of who we are. We take great pride in how we help each other. We don't use any kind of currency, unless you count respect. To be respected is the greatest achievement we can ever hope for. And to be loved. To be respected, loved and befriended. Kind of our 'holy trinity' if you will. If a Fae can achieve this within her own circle, it is almost royalty. To achieve this with a Human, I think you Humans call it 'sainthood?' Something along those lines. We 'work' side-by-side, every day. If things need to be done, they are done. Simple as that." Lila looked sad.

"I like that. I like that, a lot." Lila sighed. Nyx now looked sad. She shifted on the pillow so that she was able to prop her legs over the edge of the pillow.

"You're not happy, Lila." Before Lila could protest, Nyx said, "Work. With your, your job." Nyx was unsure of the proper wording. Lila nodded and said,

"Yes, that's right."

"Why?" Nyx asked. "Don't you like what you do? Aren't you proud of what you do?" This almost brought tears to Lila's eyes. The question hit her dead on.

"No. No, Nyx, I'm not. Not at all! I'm wasting my time. I'm wasting my money and time on a job I hate. I hate the place I work for. The people I work for are greedy, status-seeking assholes." Nyx looked down. Lila was upset. Her voice trembled and Nyx could tell the subject was a sore one. She shook her head, searching for words. They were silent for a moment. Lila collected herself and continued,

"It's my own fault. I chose not to pay attention in school; when I did show up. I absolutely hated school. I love learning and even did back then, but I just couldn't ... I didn't fit in. I had friends, many friends. I just could not think there. I felt ... smothered. The only thing that saved me was art. I love to draw. I love the feel of charcoal in my fingers. I deal with my emotions with art. It's my drug. My healing tea." Nyx nodded. "I am back in school. Art school. A crappy art school, but at least I'm going to one. I wish I could quit this horrible job and just draw for the rest of my life. I don't know. Sometimes I feel like I'm wasting my life away doing things I hate and for what?" She laughed to keep from crying. "I'm sorry." Nyx sat up.

"Close your eyes," she suggested. Lila blinked at her, quizzically. "Just do it." Lila closed them. A tear leaked from one. She sighed, wiping it away with her wrist. "Okay. Open them." Lila braced herself for what was to come. Her eyes opened. A fat blue candle was lit and on the coffee table. Next to that was a bowl of fruit, some cheese and some crackers. Next to that was her teapot, filled with what smelled of blueberries. And in her lap, a box of tissues. "I don't know about you, but I could use a snack." Lila beamed, smiling wide.

"You're amazing. You're like the best friend I have never had. How sad is that? I mean ..." She popped a raspberry into her mouth, "I have friends, but nobody I would talk like this to, though. Except for Roan. He's my best friend. But, I'm so glad you're here. I wish you could stay here all the time," Lila said. Nyx blinked as she ate a bit of cheese. She let herself grin but stopped herself from shouting cries of victory.

Later, as she flew back to the shelter behind the wall, she felt as if she might burst. *"She wants me to stay! She wants me to stay*!" She whispered over and over. She could hardly fly as tears of joy blurred her vision. She couldn't wait to tell Drake and Alva.

21

Lila cleaned up the living room and put the fruit and cheeses away. She blew the candle out and locked up. Roan would be calling soon and she thought a glass of wine would be nice. She grabbed her phone, and putting the wine on the nightstand, she slipped into clean pajamas. Cotton this time. She wasn't ill anymore and, quite frankly, it was warm. She slid the window open and a sweet cool breeze wafted in, bringing in a clean scent of rain and earth inside. *You can't bottle that.* She took a deep breath and nodded, then slid into the covers. Perfect. And right on cue, the phone rang.

"Hi, baby!" she cooed into the phone. "I am so glad you called. How are you, Love?" She heard Roan let out a long sigh.

"Baby girl." He seemed to lose his words. "I'm just so done. I'm tired. This entire thing has been such a nightmare. They do things so differently here. I've forgotten just how different this country is. I used to think that I missed it. I mean, I do. It was home for all of my childhood. Now, all I want is to come home. Home to you." He sounded sad and defeated. Lila's heart ached for him. She hated hearing him so sad.

"When can you come home? I'm sorry, Roan. I know you need to be there for Ethan. I'm being selfish. I'm just worried about you now. You must be exhausted. You'll be the next one to get sick if you're not getting enough rest, and I know you, Roan Donovan; you won't quit." He let out a grunt.

"Yeah, I know. I don't know when I can come home. There is still so much to do, even after the burial. I'm probably going to be the only one at the service. Most of his friends are back home in the States. Our old nanny is here, though. Christ, Lila, she was so broken up about his dying. She hasn't seen us since we left Ireland in 1981. She did help raise us though. She's very sweet, and very old. She gave me a few old photos of us that she had. Had them framed. I tell you, I don't know when I can get back. It might be another week because there is so much paperwork." Before he could say another word, he heard Lila let out an anguished sob.

"Shit, Roan! Another week!? Just what do you have to do, still? Isn't this stuff you can take care of via email?" She tried desperately not to let him hear her crying. Her disappointment burned through her heart. "I'm sorry, I'm sorry. I just - I just miss you so fucking bad." Now her sobs came uncontrollably.

"I know, baby. Oh, don't cry, Lila. Please. I want nothing more than to come home and snuggle with you. Lila, I've been thinking while I've been here and I really think it's time for us to move in together. I know we said that we would wait until after the wedding, but I just don't want to live without you anymore. I've seen so much sadness and despair in the past few days. It's made me really think about what's important. Life is so short, Lila, and I just want us to start living our lives together." Lila listened, tears rolling down her cheeks. "I want you with me, Lila. I hate the thought of you living alone and I honestly don't want to live alone anymore." Lila actually smirked at this. "What? Lila, what do you think?"

"Yep, I agree," she said, quickly. "I totally agree." This had always been a touchy subject between them as Roan had always wanted to live together. Lila was more traditional in her way of thinking, and she told him the last time the subject was brought up that there was no way; she wanted to begin living together after they were married. She was adamant about it. She liked being on her own. Now, all she wanted was for him to come home, to *their* home. She was truly ready to begin sharing her life with him. Suddenly, it just seemed right. "I can't wait to see you!" Her bliss was interrupted by his words.

"Hey, can you hold on for a minute? I need to ... pee. I'm sorry, Lila. I should have gone before I called." She giggled.

"Well, when you gotta go, you gotta go. Call me back?" she asked. Roan was quick to reply.

"No, just hang on. I won't be long. Please, just hang on, okay?" He sounded distracted. Lila laughed.

"Just go, already! Guess I'll go too! Pee break!" Roan laughed. She put her cell phone on the bed and quickly ran to the bathroom. She peed as fast as she could. When she finished, she washed her hands and then quickly ran to get the wine bottle on the dining room table. She ran back. She picked up her cell again.

"You back? Roan, you there? Guess you really had to go!" She hummed a little tune. She poured herself more wine, and took a sip. She slid back into the bed.

"Roan," she sing-songed into the phone, "did you fall in?" *Maybe the bathroom is far away*, she thought. She listened, squinting, trying to hear something. Anything. There was no noise on the other end. She took a sip of wine. As she swallowed, she thought she saw a shadow move just outside her bedroom window. She froze as white-hot fear stabbed her belly.

"Roan? Roan? Come on, Roan, hurry up!" she whispered urgently into the phone. She turned and as she walked toward the window, a feeling of unease seized her. She looked through the window. "Baby, please hurry!" she whispered into the phone. Suddenly, she saw a distinct shadow just to the left of her bedroom window. She gasped. Every hair on her body stood on end. "Oh shit!"

Panic filled her. Her eyes shifted to the left. She then heard what seemed to be her screen door opening, usually a comforting squeaking but now it was creepy and totally freaking her out. Taking the phone with her, she ran to the living room and stood in front of the door. As soon as she put the phone to her ear, there was a very quiet knock on her door. It was all she could do not to scream. Frozen in fear, she couldn't move. "ROAN!" she loudly whispered loudly into the phone.

"What?" Warm relief washed over her body and she felt her body relax. She heard his voice. It sounded louder than it should. Puzzled, she spoke his name again. Gathering all the courage she could find, she opened the door to find Roan standing on her porch with a huge bouquet of white roses, and a goofy grin on his face. She dropped the phone and ran into his arms.

"Roan! Oh my God! Roan! I can't believe..." She covered her mouth with both hands and her knees buckled. She knelt down involuntarily. Her heart was racing. "You sonofabitch! I thought ..." She straightened up. Roan grinned and let out a low laugh, which sent white hot sparks coursing through her body. He threw his arms around her. He could feel her heart pounding.

"Surprise!" he purred into her neck. Lila stepped back, tears streaming down her face.

"I can't believe you! I thought you were a fucking prowler, or something! I – I'm ..." Anger and fear turned into a fiery need for him. She was at a total loss for words. "Get your ass in here." She wrapped her arms around his neck and planted a passionate kiss on his lips as he laid the roses on the table. His arms pulled her to him. They kissed each other, their lips reacquainting themselves. Breaking the kiss, Lila took Roan by the hand and led him silently but quickly to her bedroom. Without words they forcefully peeled off each other's clothes and made love on the floor.

***

Roan nuzzled Lila, pulling her close to his body. He found her neck and kissed it. His voice was deep and husky in her ear,

"Why, Miss Scawlett. I do deecla-yah. Forgive me, as I'm afraid you've swept me off of my feet with your chahms," he said, his fake southern accent making her grin. He kissed her ear. Lila giggled, as she turned her body so that she was facing him. She ran her finger down his nose.

"Why, sir, you look as if," Roan smiled as Lila playfully pushed him away, "you know what I look like without my shimmy! Fiddle

Dee-Dee, Cap'n Butlah," she said with a thick fake southern drawl of her own. Her eyes squinted into an equally fake scowl, but the accent was now gone. "You scared the hell out of me, you know!" He kissed her mouth. "But I've never been so happy in all of my life. Live in sin with me. Have your way with me. Then marry me." She pulled him to her. Roan smiled at her.

"Oh, all right."

Part Two

22

"What are we going to do with three Panini makers, Lila?" Roan looked at the card accompanying each one. "I thought that was why couples registered, to avoid this? Which one should we keep? We don't even eat Panini!" Lila brought the Hefty bag into the living room and shoved the piles of balled-up wrapping paper into it. She eyed the three machines. Pointing, she quickly said,

"That one. The red one. Maybe we can sell the other two. I don't know. Let's not do this now. I'm hungry. Let's get something to eat. Wanna go out? I don't feel like cooking anything." She fell back onto the bag of tissue paper, using it as a cushion. Roan lay next to her.

"I'm hungry, too." He kissed her neck. "We don't have to cook anything." Lila closed her eyes, but her growling stomach commanded attention. "Ew, Lila!" he said, laughing. She pushed him off of her.

"Well, I said I was hungry! I don't care what we eat, but let's go somewhere. I need to get away from this mess. Just leave it." He agreed. He stood and pulled her up. Taking his keys from the dish by the door, and sliding into his leather jacket, he waited for Lila. She put on her scarf. "I'll meet you in the car. Let me get my coat and my purse, I'll be right there." He nodded and went out to warm the car up. Lila waited until she heard the car door shut. Then she went into the hallway.

"Nyx? Can you hear me? Nyx!" she whispered louder. She saw the familiar glow from behind the baseboard. Soon Nyx's tiny head peer out. She smiled brightly.

"When can we talk? I've missed you! I have so much to ask you!" Nyx replied. Lila smiled and knelt down to speak softly to her.

"I know! It's been a while and I'm so sorry! I promise the next time I can, I will call to you. We need to be very careful right now, as you know. We've just been so busy." A grin splayed across her face. Nyx grinned and stifled a giggle.

"Uh, huh! We heard. Many, many times." Lila actually felt herself blushing. "You've been very busy."

"We weren't that loud, were we?" she whispered. "Look, I have to go, but again, I just wanted to let you know that I have not forgotten about you and the others. You and I have important things we need to discuss. Maybe tomorrow night? We are going out for supper, so feel free to roam around a bit. Just be on the lookout for the car. I gotta go! Bye!" Nyx watched as Lila fled out the door. She felt a lot better now, having spoken to Lila. For the past two weeks, seeing her was by glimpses, only. Still she understood the importance of not scaring Roan. She wasn't even sure she wanted to know him. But if it pleased Lila, she would certainly try to like him. Right now, all she felt was a growing jealousy. She wanted Lila to herself and knew this was wrong. She'd talk to Drake tonight.

***

Nyx paced. She waited impatiently for Drake to finish. He was putting the finishing touches on a pair of curtains above the entrance from the hallway.

"It's so dark and drab in here! What this place needs is a splash of color here and there!" he said, smiling. He and Alva hung them up. "Oh damn! I completely forgot about the tie-backs! Well, now what?" He flew back a few feet and surveyed his work. "Yeah, I can't leave those like that. It's just plain tacky. After lunch I'll whip them up." Nyx stifled a giggle. "Well, hell, help me take them back down. Nyx? Yes, dear. I know you want to talk to me. Give me five minutes. How about you brew us up some of your fabulous anise tea?" Nyx sighed and nodded.

"Come on, Alva. Help me open these pods?" Nyx said, a tinge of annoyance ringing in her voice.

Ten minutes later, the trio sat on a large yellow satin brocade pillow (also made by Drake), and sipped anise tea. The thick aroma of licorice filled the space and seemed to have calmed the group down. The silence was, for the moment, almost as delicious as the tea. Each seemed to be deep in thought. Each had their own things to think about. Shifting her eyes from the ceiling to the pillow, Nyx broke the silence.

"Drake, I don't know if this is going to work, after all," she said quietly. He eyed her over his tea cup, his thick eyebrows pointing up.

"Hmm? What? You don't like the color, do you? Well, tell me what you want, Girl! I'm not a mind reader," he said, shaking his head. Nyx looked puzzled.

"What? What are you ..." Then she understood. "Oh! No, no. Drake, it's lovely in here! You've outdone yourself. I'm talking about staying here," she said in a whisper. "I don't know if this is something I can do anymore." Drake put his cup down.

"What do you mean?" he asked slowly.

"You know exactly what she means, Drake," Alva added. "And I, for one, agree with her. I don't like this situation anymore." Drake eyed Alva sternly. "With *him* here." Alva said. Drake's eyes turned sad.

"Well, I think it's fine. Really, I do. You just need to work a little harder. Soon he'll learn to accept you too," he said as he got up to refill his tea. He stretched his body; bones cracked. He fluffed his wings, farted, and left a puff of pink smoke behind him. "Sorry." Nyx scrunched up her nose and Alva flew to the other side of Nyx, fanning the air with her wings.

"Maybe," Nyx added, "maybe not. I mean, I just want to do this right. What if he doesn't want to live with a faerie? There are so many things that could go wrong. In the beginning, it was fine because Lila was alone and apart from that damned cat of hers, things were going so well."

Drake poured tea for the two of them as Alva was prepared a light supper. "Dearie, you still need to have a talk with Lila. You need to get her to tell you about Roan, and not about what kind of tea he likes either. You need to learn how he feels about mystical things. I've learned that if men believe in what they call the 'paranormal', then you're just about set." The looks on the other two Fae made him stop. "Human men are funny creatures. They don't like to show their inner selves that much. It's not 'manly' to do so. Totally ridiculous, yes." Alva turned and looked at the two of them, stirring the big pot of stew.

"Paranormal? What's that?" she asked. Drake downed his tea. Stifling a burp, he began.

"Ah. Paranormal: beyond the range of normal experience or scientific explanation. Pertaining to the claimed occurrence of an event or perception without scientific explanation, as psycho-kinesis, extrasensory perception, or other purportedly supernatural phenomena." The looks on the women's faces irritated him. "You know; the unexplained. Ghosts and apparitions. All that scary shit the Humans like to watch on television." Nyx nodded. Alva looked scared and went back to stirring her stew. Drake continued, "If people believe in this stuff, a belief in something like, say, faeries, isn't so far-fetched. It might be odd, but they already have an open mind to things they cannot see or explain, so it's easier to believe in - us. And Human women seem to accept this easier than Human men do. Does that make any sense?" To Nyx, it really did. She smiled.

"Totally. That makes perfect sense." Drake put his chubby arm around her.

"Good." He put his thick glasses on and went back to his sewing kit.

"And what if he doesn't believe in ghosts or apparitions? In the supernatural?" Nyx said under her breath. "Then what?"

23

Lila slammed the phone down. She put her head into her hands. She could feel her pulse in her temples. *Why can't people do something as simple as counting? So fucking stupid.* She took off her glasses and rubbed her eyes. Now, she would have to tell her supervisor that the counts were not only off, but totally off. How can a person mistake twenty-thousand for twenty? Those three extra zeros didn't do it? She was amazed at the amount of stupidity that was employed here. And, of course, this would somehow end up being all her fault, just like it always did. Her stomach was growling and she needed to get away. She logged out of the system and grabbed her purse. "I need go get out of here. Be back in an hour," she said to whoever heard her. She really didn't care. She went to a sub shop and bought a chicken salad on rye and a sparkling water. She ate in the car.

Her thoughts turned to Nyx. She really missed her. It had been so long since they last spoke and she felt so bad about not being able to sit and talk. Roan would be going out of town for a night.

"Tomorrow, Nyxie. I promise!" She made a mental note to somehow slip her a note telling her to plan to come out and spend the evening with her. She drove back to the office and went straight to her boss's office and shut the door. It would probably get loud and heated.

She watched Roan twirl the spaghetti around his fork. She grinned. Once upon a time, she would watch in horror as he cut his noodles with a knife into tiny pieces. She told him if he was going to be a part of her life, he would have to stop doing that and to twirl his pasta properly. The last straw was when she accompanied him to his annual Christmas Eve office dinner and watched him cut it. It actually turned into an argument in the parking lot.

"How do you eat spaghetti at Mama Regina's and cut your spaghetti!? You might as well just spit in her food!" she had yelled. *"My last name is Irish, too, but I do have some Italian in me. Don't do that again."* He didn't. Now it was second nature. She watched him suck a noodle into his mouth. As hungry as he was, he didn't notice her watching him. A drop of marinara splashed onto his cheek. He didn't notice that, either. She let out a silent laugh. Chewing, he looked up at her and smiled. This made her laugh out loud.

"Here!" She handed him a napkin, he took it and nodded, wiping his lips. He crumpled the napkin and set it next to his plate. He looked at her, stopping mid-chew.

"What?" he asked. She smiled and tapped her cheek. "Oh." He cleaned his cheek. "Better?" She silently nodded. Sighing, she put her fork down.

"I'll eat later." She pushed her plate away. Her grin fading, she stared at the salt shaker, lost in thought. She felt Roan's fingers touch her hand.

"Bad day?" He poured them both some wine. "Wanna talk about it?" She nodded. "Come on, let's go sit in the living room." She followed him. He took the end of the sofa and put one leg across it and let the other rest on the floor. He patted the empty spot in front of him. She smiled and sat against him. He handed her glass to her as she nuzzled close to his body. She let herself lie back and rested her head against his chest. Roan then wrapped his legs around her body. "Okay. Now, tell Roan all about it. What happened?" She told him all about her day. The frustration. She told him how unhappy she was there. Soon she was spilling her heart out to him. She felt like there was nowhere to go, no way to advance.

"I wish I could just quit and go to art school. I know; that's so damned selfish of me." He kissed her hair. He sighed. She smelled spaghetti and grimaced. Still, she felt good. She sipped her wine.

"Lila, if you're really that unhappy, then quit. We'll be okay for a while. Just quit. Focus on your classes. There is temp work, you know. Why not look into that?" She let out a breath.

"That's true. I can't just quit though. We need the money! I have tuition, a car payment, electric!" She said. In her secret heart of hearts, she was hoping Roan would tell her again that it would be fine if she quit. She got her wish.

"I can't see how being miserable could be healthy. You're stressed out. I can see it. Baby, go in there tomorrow, give your two weeks with a smile and a thank you. Or, just tell them to shove the job straight up their asses, to have a nice day, and be done with it. Don't worry about expenses. We can manage." She shifted and kissed his mouth. His hand slid into her blouse and touched her. The night ended perfectly and sweetly.

24

In an odd way, it felt really good. Lila felt as if a heavy wet blanket had been pulled off of her back. She had gone into her boss's office and, putting on her best sad face, gave her two weeks' notice. She reiterated just how sorry she was to have to do this, but sudden life changes were forcing her to quit. Her boss had other ideas though, and fired her on the spot. At first, Lila was shocked; wanting to quit was one thing. Getting fired stung a little. After listening to her boss's verbal vomit about Lila's lack of dedication and inability to multitask, Lila smiled, nodded and with a sharp snap of her fingers said,

"Yeah, whatever. Oh, kiss my fat ass." As she walked out, her head held high, one of her co-workers gave her a smile and a thumbs up. Lila walked over to her and hugged her, then never looked back.

She felt free.

Usually a Tuesday night would see another evening of preparing for a day of work. For Lila, it was, for now at least, a time to stretch, linger and enjoy time without stress. She shed a tear as she waved goodbye to Roan as he left for Baltimore. She truly would miss him. She was glad that his trip would be just overnight. She drove home smiling though. Tonight she had plans. She really didn't like sneaking around behind his back, but when she really thought about it, she was doing absolutely nothing wrong! *It's not like I'm having an affair, or something.* This would be a topic she would have to bring up with Nyx. First though, a happy reunion.

The night was very cold, so she decided to build a fire. When she arrived home, the house was already warm, with a roaring fire already ablaze. Wonderful aromas greeted her. There was a lovely garland made of clover, pine, and lilac (for Lila) draping perfectly around the hearth. She hung her coat in the closet and took off her boots, placing them on the stone hearth to dry. Nyx flew out and landed on her shoulder, getting lost in Lila's curls. The two of them giggled. Nyx untangled herself and flew in front of Lila's face.

"Welcome home! Now, first. Go have a bath. It's waiting for you. I will meet you there in a few minutes." She kissed Lila's cheek then darted away toward the kitchen. Lila quickly walked into the bedroom. There she found her favorite blue robe clean and waiting for her. She undressed and slid into it. It was softer than she ever remembered it could be and smelled faintly like clover. She inhaled deeply. Smiling, she walked into her bathroom.

Blue candles were lit again. The aroma was intoxicating, but not overpowering. Fluffy towels and a washcloth were placed on the sink. On the stool was a steaming cup of tea. The tub was filled with pale blue water and bubbles floated on top. A huge bouquet of carnations sat in an old washbasin. She slid out of the robe and tested the water with her toe. Again, the water seemed way too hot for her, but as she slid in, it enveloped her like a familiar soft blanket. Or a comforting hug. She sank into the water, letting her head and face sink under its depths. *If only I could breathe in here, I'd never leave!* She emerged with bubbles on her head. She heard giggles. Wiping the suds away, she opened her eyes to find Nyx lying on the fluffy towel, watching her.

"Nice, huh?" she asked. Lila nodded, eyes closed. All she could do was nod. "Good. Supper is simmering. Morel soup. Bitter green salad. For desert, chocolate cake with honey sugar." Lila smiled. "Hey! See that there by the stool? On the floor. The bubbles!" Lila leaned toward the edge of the tub, water sloshing over her breasts. Open it and blow a big bubble," Nyx said. She looked like a little kid. Lila smiled.

"Wow. I haven't blown bubbles since I was ten!" Lila said as she quickly unscrewed the bottle. This one had a bubble wand already attached to the lid. She quickly blew a stream of little bubbles. Nyx clapped and squeaked with glee. Lila laughed. "Oh, this brings back so many memories!" She blew more and then Nyx sat up.

"Hey. Blow a big one." Lila grinned. She blew one as Nyx watched. It sailed over the tub, over Nyx's head and popped on the mirror. "Blow another one. Bigger, this time!" Lila dunked the wand into the bottle and slowly blew into the ring. A large bubble formed. It bobbled and colors formed, swirling around it. It finally detached from the wand, hovering for a second, then suddenly Nyx leapt off of the towel and flew toward it. Lila stared at the scene and dared not move. "Watch, now." And in a flash, Nyx was inside the bubble. She sat inside it and it hovered right next to Lila's knee. She giggled. "Betcha wish you could do this, huh?" Lila looked with wonder, a grin splaying across her face. The colors of the bubble swirled madly around it, greens, pinks, deep blues and greens. Nyx took a deep breath and blew with all her might. Now, the colors changed, swirling faster around, and the bubble rose up.

"Wow. Just like Glinda in the *Wizard of Oz*," she whispered dreamily, watching the bubble rise above her. Nyx frowned.

"Who is Glinda?" She said, but then blew more air. She floated up near the bathroom window. Lila smirked.

"You know! Glinda, the Good Witch. *The Wizard of Oz*?" Lila followed the bubble's path with her eyes.

"You know a witch," Nyx said, turning around excitedly,"...and a wizard?" The bubble began its descent. Nyx sat again as Lila watched in awe. Lila shook her head then held up a soapy index finger.

"No," she laughed. "It's a story; a faerie tale." Nyx glared at Lila, then giggled. The bubble landed on Lila's finger. "It's a movie. Someday we'll watch it." They both giggled again and enjoyed this interlude while it lasted. Lila gently put the bubble back onto the towel where it popped. Nyx quickly covered her eyes.

"Can you please turn this towel over? It 's all soapy, now." Lila happily obliged and then relaxed in the tub.

"We need to talk, Nyx." Lila said sweetly to her. Nodding, Nyx agreed.

25

Sitting on the floor in front of the fire, Nyx and Lila ate the morel soup Nyx prepared. It was, in a word, exquisite. Creamy and buttery, with the sharp twang of wild morel mushrooms, deep earthy flavor adding to the euphoria of the sweet butter and cream. Lila had never tasted anything like it. They ate in silence. Nyx cleared her throat.

"Tell me about Roan," she said, "First, tell me about how you fell in love with him." Her eyes took a glow from the fire that added to their already dreamy gaze. Lila grinned.

"Everything?" She asked, licking her spoon. She ladled more of the creamy soup into her bowl. Nyx pushed her tiny bowl away and made a place to recline. Lila suddenly had an idea. "Hey, wait! Don't move. I'll be right back." She got up and ran into her bedroom. She opened the closet door and tugged on the chain to turn on the light. Searching, she found her old doll house. A tiny bean bag chair made out of purple satin and filled with seed beads she had made when she was eleven. Perfect! She dusted it off and brought it into the living room. Nyx flew up and kissed Lila. Lila nodded.

"Comfy?" Nyx snuggled into the tiny chair, her arms behind her head and her legs dangling off of the side. She looked like a love-struck teenager. She thanked Lila.

"Come on! I want to hear about ..." Nyx pondered for a moment, "your first date! Tell me all about your first date with Roan!" She settled in and waited like a child getting ready to hear her favorite bedtime story. Lila too thought for a moment. Her eyes glinted. A knowing grin appeared. "Yeah, "Nyx said, seductively. "Tell me about that; about whatever made you blush like that!" Lila shot Nyx a warning look, but then she softened. Her eyes wandered to the fire.

"Let me see," Lila began. "Although I had asked Roan out, it was he who decided what we would do. I was pretty much up for anything..."

"Hi! Wow, you look great!" Lila smiled brightly. She looked at Roan and thanked him.

"I guess we both got the blue & white memo, huh?" The couple looked at each other's clothing; Lila in a white sundress with blue flowers. Roan in jeans with a blue and white seersucker. Roan nodded, letting out a laugh.

"I guess we did! Well, all that means is that we are certain to have a great time." His eyes took her in. Driving down Coastal Highway 1, Roan and Lila discussed possible places to go, deciding on Fins. Fins was a little place right on the beach, with a nice bar, great food, and decorated with both kinds of fins: tropical fish and old cars. Huge freshwater aquariums lined the

restaurant, and the actual fins of old Chryslers and Cadillacs decorated some of the booths. It was still quite early, so there wasn't a line to get in. Roan and Lila decided to have a drink at the bar.

Lila sipped her Margarita. She didn't want to drink a lot. She wanted to keep a sharp and clear mind. She looked at Roan, taking him in. Hazel eyes and lashes longer than hers. Eyes she could easily get lost in. His dark brown hair was too long; growing out of a cut. His hair was probably too long by most women's standards, but on Roan, it was beautiful, it was very refreshing seeing a man who truly took care of his hair. She envisioned brushing it; running her hands through it. It was gorgeous. She had to make herself stop staring at him. When she did get to glance at him, she marveled at the little things that made him so handsome. She wanted to sit at a table instead of the bar. It was all she could do to not keep looking at him. As if Roan could read her mind, he asked her if she would like to get a table. They took one near one an aquarium.

They decided to order dinner as well. Lila surprised herself and ate heartily. Normally, she was self-conscious about eating on first dates, but the conversation was so good and Roan was so interesting, she relaxed and had no qualms about it. Roan ordered another round of drinks and suggested that they sit on one of the tables overlooking the ocean. Roan sat silently looking Lila. The moonlight plus the candle on the table gave just enough light to illuminate the two of them. Roan smiled at Lila. He looked at her hand.

"What a pretty ring," he said, and looked at the silver and onyx ring. Lila smiled back.

"Thanks. My father gave it to me on my eighteenth birthday. I wear it all the time; I never take it off." Roan fingered the smooth, black stone. Lila watched Roan's eyes as he let his fingers touch hers. He gently took her hand in his. Lila felt her insides burn. She looked into Roan's eyes again. She wanted to feel this way for so long. "It's wonderful to feel this good and so alive." She thought to herself. Roan was enjoying her, as well. He knew she was enjoying herself, but also realized that she needed time. Lila took her hand away and sipped her drink. Before they knew it, the bar had called for last call and was shutting down.

It seemed as if only an hour had passed. Roan paid the tab and asked Lila if she would like to take a short walk on the beach. They strolled along, sharing little tidbits of their lives. Their hands brushed each other. Lila decided to take the initiative; she hooked Roan's pinkie finger in hers, swinging it in time with their slow stride. He looked at her, his hair blowing wildly in the sea breeze, and even in the darkness, she could feel his eyes on her. His finger tightened around hers.

"I just love the night ocean air." Her own hair now slapped her face. She used her other hand to brush it away, but he turned toward her, and using his right hand, brushed it away himself. He tucked it behind her ear. As he did this, his pinkie released hers and his hand held hers. "It's so long!" he said, smiling. She blushed. "It's beautiful." he said softly. She tingled. She felt as she were glowing, afraid he could see it. They continued walking, darting away from the incoming tide.

"Thank you. I love the ocean air, too. It cleanses the soul." She let the ocean breeze blow her hair, tilting her head back. She could feel his eyes on her again. She looked at him and sure *enough, he was looking. A sideways glance that sent sparks throughout her body. He inhaled deeply. Finally he said the words she dreaded.*

"Well, it's getting very late. I'm sorry. I didn't realize it was this late. I should get you home."

Lila agreed, although she hated hearing him say it. They walked slowly back to his car, savoring every minute together. Roan opened the car door and Lila slid in. The car smelled like Roan, Ivory soap and the sea. A nice mix. She inhaled deeply, hoping that the scent would stay with her after he dropped her off. Roan got in and started the engine. He looked at Lila. He smiled. Lila smiled back. Roan's intense stare made her giggle. Nervously, she asked,

"Um, is something wrong?" her heart pounding. She was sure he could hear it! He continued looking at her. He ran his hand through his hair. It fell perfectly into place. Later, Lila would learn that this gesture was one he did whenever he was nervous. He replied,

"No, not a thing. I-I just like looking at you. I'm sorry. I'm making you uncomfortable." He looked down then back at Lila. Although Lila blushed, she added:

"It's - It's okay, I just thought something was, never mind. I, uh, like looking at you, too."

If ever there was a moment in her life where she wanted to crawl under a rock and die, this was would have been the one. She shook her head. Roan looked at her and smiled. "God," she said, laughing in spite of herself. "I'm such a dork." Roan's glance sweetened.

"No, you're not," he said softly.

The drive home was quiet. Each was dreading having to part. Still, the ride was nice. As they made their way back to Lila's house, Roan asked her if she'd like to go out again sometime. She happily accepted. She asked him if he'd be interested in having dinner at her place after she got back home from school some night. They made plans to arrange a day. They arrived at Lila's door.

"I had a really good time, tonight, Roan," she said, leaning on the wooden railing. Roan faced her.

"So did I, Lila. I'm looking forward to seeing you again." Lila felt her insides burn and she knew this night must end soon, as much as she wanted it to go on. Roan gazed into her eyes. He moved a bit closer to her. She could have just drowned in that hazel pool. Roan moved even closer.

"Lila?" his voice was soft and deep. His full lips shone in the moonlight. She already loved those lips.

"Yes?" she said, her voice quavering. Roan tilted his head.

"Can I tell you something?" he asked as Lila stepped toward him. His finger touched her hand. The hairs on her arms stood up.

"Uh-huh, sure." Roan moved his head close to Lila's as his fingers now grazed hers. She could feel the heat of his skin. His hand then left hers. Again his voice purred.

"I'm dying to kiss you." He was so close now, that Lila could feel him even though they were not touching. She moved closer to him. Her reply was barely audible.

"Hmm. Really?" Her fingers brushed his arm. Roan's face was within inches of hers. He replied, his voice just a breeze with sound,

"Really," he said as he looked into her eyes. Lila sucked in her breath. She felt his hands slide up her bare arms up to her shoulders. Roan's lips were only a breath away from hers. She swallowed.

"Well, what are we going to do about this?" Lila asked, trembling. Their eyes locked, lips about to make contact.

Roan whispered onto her,

"I don't know."

Roan lightly brushed his full lips onto Lila's. She returned the favor. It was if neither of them wanted to rush; this was a moment to be savored. Almost as if a full-blown kiss would have ruined the moment. They both continued this playful exchange, slowly letting their lips play and get to know each other. Eventually lingering longer locking into a sweet kiss. Roan's arms embraced Lila's waist and Lila's arms encircled Roan's neck. Her hands finally slid through his silky soft hair. Lila felt Roan's mouth open and his tongue darted slowly onto her upper lip, as if asking permission. Lila responded by darting out hers and licking the underside of Roan's tongue, deepening their kiss even more. Lila, with all her might, slowly pulled away. Roan rested his head on her forehead. The couple let their breathing settle. Roan kissed her forehead,

"I should go. I'll call you tomorrow, okay?" Lila, straightened herself and tried to stand without her knees giving way.

"Ok. Drive safely, Roan." He kissed her hand.

"Sweet dreams, Lila."

"Wow! That's *so* romantic! I'm all tingly!" Nyx was now lying on her belly, chin in hand. She looked at Lila dreamily. "You're so lucky. I want that." The two talked into the wee hours of the morning. Lila was amused by Nyx's interest in love and sex. She wasn't sure if she should start toning it down or let herself scream with abandon about her sex life with Roan. Nyx tried hard to explain how Fae express physical love, but it was not so cut and dry. "Fae become one, but not truly in the literal sense that Humans do. That is one thing I simply can't share with you, Lila. It's sacred. We express love our in similar ways, but they are very different from yours. Just as intense, and perhaps even more so. Our coming together in love does involve our forms, but on a more creative level," she said. Seeing confusion on Lila's face she simply didn't explain further other than to say, "We love too."

Lila took a call from Roan in her bedroom. He had a way of speaking to her that made her feel as if she had just come home from that first date with him. It was all she could do not to hop on a plane to Baltimore right now, but her saving grace was that he would be home by this time tomorrow night. She came back into the living room. A slice of chocolate cake with honey sugar was waiting for her. Lila dipped her finger into the frosting and tasted it. Not surprisingly, it was delicate yet decadent. They ate the sweet cake in silence. Then Lila began.

"How do we approach Roan?" she asked. "I honestly don't know how to go about this." Nyx returned to her bean-bag chair.

"I was discussing this with Alva and Drake, who by the way, wish to meet you as soon as possible, and they both agree that we should find out how he feels about odd things. The paranormal. Would you know?" Lila thought about it. She honestly had no idea. The subject had never come up.

"Funny, but I have no clue. I am a total believer, myself," Lila admitted. Nyx nodded, not surprised. "I'll have to bring it up. Why do you ask?"

"Well, we believe that if a person - a Human - believes in such things, then seeing one of us might not be so shocking. Lila, do you want Roan to know about me?" Nyx asked, biting a nail. For the first time, Lila was at a loss for words. For a split second, she wanted to say, "No." "You don't, do you." A sadness came over Nyx that she was not prepared for. Tears dropped from her eyes. Lila shifted on the rug.

"What would you think if I said that I didn't?" Lila asked, gently. "What's so wrong with not telling him. What if he didn't believe me? He could think I'm losing my marbles and commit me." She saw that Nyx looked puzzled. She thought for a moment. "Hmm, committed, it means if you lose your mind, or are deemed unstable or crazy, you could be sent to a place where you live in a medicated state, a zombie-like state, for the rest of your life." Nyx looked terrified.

"But you're not like that!" But before Nyx could continue, Lila added,

"How many Humans do you see hanging out with a pixie, Nyx? In our world?" Nyx was speechless. "Exactly! I'll need to really feel Roan out and see how he thinks." Lila poked at the dwindling fire. It was very late now. She felt uneasy. There was a very good possibility that Roan either would not accept Nyx, or think Lila was nuts. This could very well ruin their marriage. Roan was a part of her now and as much as she loved the idea of sharing not only her home but also her life with another living being, she was not willing to lose her husband. "I still think that, given time and a bit of cautious effort, we could pull this off. I mean, who wouldn't want to meet and live with a faerie!? Shit, maybe it'd send him over the edge. What if he lost it after seeing or meeting you? What if he couldn't handle it? Maybe Roan would be the one wearing the straight-jacket in his own rubber room. I can't think anymore." The two hugged a long time, Nyx leaning against Lila's fingers. Lila, despite the odd conversation, really enjoyed the evening.

"It's like your date with Roan. 'Can I see you again?' 'I had a great time!' But I did, Lila. I have to be honest; I am doing all I can to make this house my new home. I am perfectly content living behind the wall. All I truly want is to be your friend, and to make sure you're safe and happy." She darted up to Lila's face and planted and a tiny kiss on her cheek. She then turned and flew back into the hall and disappeared behind the baseboard. Lila's tears made the emerald path glitter even brighter.

26

Lila sat cross-legged on the floor. She scrubbed the paper with her paper tortillion, blending the ragged graphite strokes into a smooth layer. This was homework that she loved to do. Her assignment, and current subject of study, was drawing objects that were transparent, glass and crystal. Windows. Water or other clear liquids. Most of her classmates groaned and complained when the instructor gave the assignment. It really was a difficult task; it's not easy to draw what you don't see and not draw what you think you see. Still, she grinned at her instructor as she left the classroom. She chose a difficult piece. She had a piece of cardboard and used masking tape to mark areas on it to set up her still-life of an empty wet drinking glass with a wet spoon next to it. She marked a spot on her window where the sun would be (or the point of greatest light if it was cloudy). She was in a great mood. A good night's sleep did wonders for her doubtful mind. Good tea helped. She bopped her head in time with the music. Feeling nostalgic, she put on a Shaun Cassidy album. She was still a fan.

She didn't care who made fun of her either. His music made her happy.

Dinner was already simmering in the crockpot, beef stew. Engrossed in drawing, she didn't hear Roan's car pull up. He found her hunched over her large sketchpad on the floor. The sound of his keys made her turn around. She smiled.

"Hi!" She followed his eyes as he knelt down to her level and planted a kiss on his mouth. He nuzzled her head and inhaled.

"You smell so good. What's that?" He asked as he turned the volume on the old turntable down. "Homework?" Lila nodded.

"Yeah. I think it's coming along okay. We have to show how light and shadow can make something transparent have depth." He looked over it then looked up at the objects on the table.

"You know, you could just take a photo and use it for reference." She stood, wiping her graphite covered fingers on a paper towel.

"I know, and we could have, but we get extra credit if we actually 'follow the light.' And, I already took a photo." Giggling, she opened a manila folder and produced an eight by ten. She then put her supplies away and washed her hands in the kitchen. Roan came up behind her and slid his arms around her belly, pulling her tightly to him. He kissed her neck. Rinsing her hands, Lila smiled. She then leaned her head back. "How was your day?"

"Weird," he said with a scowl. He released her and washed his own hands. "One of the kids made a naughty comic. Lila, this thing was so scary! Who knew teenagers could think up this kind of shit. Makes you wonder where mom and dad are. He had this poor woman being raped by aliens. Crazy kid."

Instantly, Lila's mind went to Nyx. Before she knew it, she was defending the kid. "You don't know why he did that. Maybe he saw it. Maybe he believes in it." Roan lifted the lid to the crockpot and sniffed. Roan shook his head.

"I believe in Humans and animals, but I'd never draw someone fucking a cat." Lila gasped.

"Oh, my God! Roan, that's just disgusting. You know exactly what I meant! I meant that he's just showing his creative side. Okay, so it's scary. What's so wrong with a story about Humans and aliens having sex? It's a story. Make-believe!" Roan wasn't having it.

"The boy drew an alien having sex with a cat, Lila. I should let you thumb through it. I had to confiscate it. Lila, this was worse than any crazy porn I've ever watched." Shaking his head, he unbuttoned his shirt. "I'm going to go do some grading." He kissed her cheek and left the kitchen.

***

Roan sat in the second bedroom at his desk. They both decided that, for the time being, it would be Roan's study. It was cramped, but until they could afford to buy a bigger house, this would do. He was on his laptop grading papers. He taught high school computer animation and Drawing I and Drawing II. He loved his job. Art and kids, two things he loved. He was still young enough to truly get through to them, too. The kids, for the most part, loved him.

Music is also art. I allow music of all kinds in this class, as long as we share the genres. Bring in a CD of your choice. Each of you will be able to play it during class. No headphones are welcome in this class, no IPods either. If I see them, they're mine until the end of the quarter. I want all of you to experience different kinds of music. If you like or dislike it, it won't matter. What matters is that you will be able to channel it out if you are engrossed in your art.

At first, this plan didn't seem to work. But as the weeks wore on, it became interesting to see what the students would play. When the captain of the wrestling team gave him a CD of Vivaldi's *Four Seasons*, he knew he was onto something. Plus, it was a great way to hear some new or unfamiliar music, not just for the kids, but for him too.

He pulled the sketch books from his backpack. He found the one he told Lila about. He opened it up to the current submission. His assignment had been for the kids to create a two-page comic; he didn't really care what the story was about, but two things were expected: the comic had to be drawn in pen and ink. No computer graphics this time, and each cell had to use a horizon line and one cell must use three, four, or five-point perspective. The kid was an amazing artist; it was just the actual story that was so disturbing. Thinking about what Lila had said earlier, however, he decided to give it another read. While he still had to confiscate it (and if he played by the rules, report it to not only his superiors, but also to the boy's parents), he wanted to read it again from an artistic point of view. He also tried to see Lila's side. While he could not let her read it, he could still take her views into account.

Lila peeked into the room. "Try to see beyond the pornographic stuff. That's all I'm saying." She winked, turned on a heel and was gone. She knew he was re-reading the comic. She hoped he could see past the taboo themes. Or perhaps she was just totally crazy and had no true idea what the story told. Still, she knew how he dealt with this could most likely tell her how she should proceed next.

Lila lay across their bed, reading. She sipped peach tea. The room was warm with the aroma. Hitch lay curled at her feet, snoring away. She heard the shower turn off and soon Roan entered the room with a black towel wrapped around his waist. She looked up at him and smiled. His chest glistened with beads of water. She watched him dry off and put his favorite flannel pajamas on. He looked at himself in the mirror on the dresser. He scratched his new beard. "I like it," Lila said, closing the book. "It's rugged." Roan examined himself, opening his mouth wide then closing it.

"It's itchy, but I might let it grow." He ran a comb through his wet hair. He was tired and knew Lila would want to discuss the comic. "Babe, I'm beat. Mind if I just try to get some sleep? Let's sleep in and go out to breakfast in the morning. We could go into town and walk it off afterwards. And talk." He slid next to her. "I'm sorry. It's been a hell of a crazy day. I promise we'll talk tomorrow." He kissed her forehead. She closed her eyes, yawing.

"Yeah. I'm tired too." They slid under the blankets. She turned onto her side and she felt his body slide close, cupping hers. His arm snaked around her waist. If they both hadn't been so tired, it would have been a sweet way to initiate something. Before she could hold his hand, though, they were both sound asleep.

Breakfast was good. Croissants and coffee. They went up the coastal highway heading north until they reached the little French café that stood just outside the little shopping district. They sat outside, wrapped in scarves, and people watched as they lingered over coffee and pastries. It was cold, but with the candle on the table and padded chairs, it was very comforting. Roan, as he always did, brought his camera with him. He took photos of their meal. Of Lila. Of Lila sipping coffee. Of the tourists and shoppers. Soon they were walking toward Main Street. Quaint shops lined both sides of the cobblestone street. Smoke shops and antique stores. Vintage clothing and aromatherapy shops. Bead stores and, ironically, a comic book store. Grinning, they walked into McKenna's Cosmic Comics.

It was tiny and musty, smelling of moldy books. Somehow, that just added to it's ambience. The walls were plastered with posters of comic book heroes, both known and new to them. They browsed the narrow shelves and aisles. Old familiar favorites were found by both of them; Roan grabbed a vintage *Spider Man* that he swore he used to have as a kid, and Lila found two: an old *Banana Splits*, and a classic *Nancy And Sluggo*. Toward the back of the shop was another room, separated by a tacky beaded curtain. An obviously hand written sign read:

Absolutely no one under 18 permitted beyond this point. Proper ID required.

Looking back, the guy at the counter didn't seem at all interested in checking IDs or who went beyond the beaded curtain. They proceeded through. At first glance, the comic books seemed just like the others outside the room, like the ones in the bookstores. A closer look, however, told a different story.

Scantily-clad women with weapons. Obvious sexual undertones. The two parted and browsed through the books. Lila picked one up simply called *Hardcore Toonz*. Based on the cover, that was an understatement. Page after page of porn in comic form. As she browsed, she noticed that while some of the comics were meant for nothing but masturbation, some were actually very well done. Some were, quite frankly, beautifully executed. Yes, it was blatant sex, but this one actually had a story to it. It was art! She read through it as Roan browsed the more hardcore section. He picked up *Bullets and Booty*.

"Do people actually spend time drawing this stuff and writing stories to it?" He whispered to Lila. She didn't hear him. He put the book back and walked to where she was reading. He stood next to her and peeked at what she was looking at. She stopped reading.

"Here; a perfect example to what I was trying to get across to you yesterday." He took the book from her and flipped through it. He began reading. He flipped more, looking at the drawings. This book was called *The Lost*. Basically, it was the same storyline that his student wrote about, without the blatant nastiness. This was exquisite. He flipped through it and seemed impressed. "I'll get it for you if you want," he whispered. Lila smiled, nodding.

"We can read it later." She winked and walked back through the beads to the cash register.

***

"But you now see what I was trying to say, right?" Lila said as she chopped leeks. "There is a market for that stuff, Roan. Like it or not, it is an art form." She put the leeks into the food processor and added chicken broth. "Now, getting back to the alien-human thing," She thought she'd would just dive right into the subject, and see where things went. She hoped he would have a more open mind than she was beginning to think he had.

Sitting down at the dining room table, she passed Roan the soup tureen. She took the plate of bread from Roan and swallowed. "Let me ask you a question," she started, matter-of-factly. He nodded. "Do you believe in the paranormal?" Roan looked at her while he ladled soup into his bowl. His eyebrows knit upwards. He shrugged. Lila tried a different tactic. "I mean, do you believe in things you sometimes can't explain?" He shook his head.

"That *would* be the paranormal. I know what it means, babe," he said, a tinge of irritation in his voice. She frowned, insulted ."I don't really know. I guess I want to believe. Like what? You mean like ghosts?" he asked. Lila shrugged.

"Yeah, I guess," she said, buttering a roll. She shrugged, trying to seem non-complacent. "Ghosts, poltergeists, spirits? Maybe even beyond that. UFOs?" Roan looked up from his soup, wiping his beard with a napkin.

"I saw one once. I swear to God, Babe! I was camping with my dad. I was about sixteen or seventeen." Roan's demeanor changed instantly. He spoke with an intense clarity as if he needed to truly convey what he felt to Lila. Pushing the bowl away, he continued. "And we were night fishing. Dad and I went to Messalonskee Lake every fall to fish. It's amazing up there." Lila finished her soup, listening. "It was getting really cold, so dad went back to the car to get some matches to start our fire. It was really dark because, obviously, it's really secluded up at Messalonskee. I mean it was so dark that unless the moon was out or you had a fire going, you couldn't see your hand in front of you. It was just like that. The stars were everywhere." Roan's voice suddenly took on a dreamy tone. "Just jillions of 'em. We had a flashlight, and dad used it to get to the car. It was parked a ways away; we had to hike a bit to reach our camping spot. That's when I saw something weird shoot across the sky over the lake. It was like a silvery blue triangle with blinking lights all around it. Lila, it didn't make a sound! Totally silent. It went by so fast but then it just kind of stopped and hovered by the edge of the tree line at the other side of the lake. It was still very far out. Then, out of the blue it just... disappeared. It disappeared, Lila, vaporized into nothing! I stood there wondering what had happened. I actually shook my head to make sure I wasn't seeing things! I was so God-dammed scared," he said, shaking his head. To Lila, it looked as if Roan was too scared to continue, but his eyes met hers. He crumpled his napkin and started tearing it apart as he spoke again. "I was speechless. I knew if I told my dad, he'd have thought I was smoking something. I never said a word to anyone about it, but the next day, while we were at the bait shop, I overheard this old guy talking. He said he'd seen *that thing* again. 'Goddamned thing shot straight across the water, just like it did five years ago. I nearly wet myself.' I tried to listen. I wanted to hear what he said, but dad was already out the door." Lila's eyes were huge. "The whole time I watched that thing, Lila, I couldn't breathe. I couldn't blink. Like it had a kind of ... hold on me." He shivered.

"Why didn't you ever tell me about that?   That's incredible," she said in a whisper. She waited for him to add something, but when he didn't, she took a breath and asked him, "Now, the question is, do you really think it was a UFO?" Lila asked this with as much care as she could express. "I'm not doubting you at all. You know, I think I'm gonna need some wine for this conversation," she added as Roan fiddled with his napkin. He nodded.

"I totally agree." He waited for her to return with the wine. She poured him his then sat down, pouring herself a full glass. She looked at Roan. He lifted his glass toward her. "To the unknown." He winked and toasted. She nodded, letting her glass kiss his. She sipped, locking the toast, eyeing him. The wine warmed her chest as it went down. He swallowed and continued, "Oh, and, just for the record, I know it was a UFO. It had to be. Nothing else that I've ever seen, Lila, could have done what I saw this thing do. I mean, it just sailed above the lake, hovered for a while then it was gone. Lila, I'm telling you ... it was far away, but I could definitely make out a shape. Nothing our Air Force makes looks like that, and if it does, I've never seen it." Lila sipped again, but looked at him, confused.

"I dunno, Roan. Our military is full of secrets. Aviary secrets. It could have been some new test plane." But Roan wasn't having it. He shook his head.

"No way. Lila, that thing fucking disappeared into nothing right before my eyes. I wasn't drunk, and I wasn't high or tired or sleepy. I was wide awake and sober. I didn't blink. I couldn't! That fucking thing up and disappeared like a fart in the wind." The look on his face suddenly worried her; this, his telling her all of this, was obviously bringing back some bad memories for him. He looked uneasy sitting there now. Lila pushed her chair out and went to Roan, hugging him. He was shaking and trying to hide it. She kissed his head, and then knelt down in front of him, taking his hands into hers.

"I believe you. Roan, do you understand? I am not doubting you at all. I totally believe you, okay? I totally believe that there is something out there. There just has to be." She ran her fingers through his long hair, brushing it away from his face. He blinked back tears, looking at her intensely, embarrassed. He wiped them away with his hand. Nodding,

"Hell, yeah. I know there is. Thanks. I'm sorry, Honey. I haven't told anyone this story; story. Shit, it's no story. It happened. I haven't told a soul about this until tonight." He laughed nervously and downed the rest of his wine. He poured them both another tall glass. Lila felt bad, now. Roan patted her hand. "I'm fine, baby, really," he promised, and pulled her to him and hugged her close. She had one last question for him. Gathering all of her courage,

"One more thing. Do you *want* to believe what you saw? Do you want to believe that there are things out there, somewhere beyond our reach, beyond explanation, that we have no proof of actually existing? Or would you rather think, 'If it can't be seen, it doesn't exist'? Do you want to see the unknown?" He let go of her hand. He took his wine glass and guzzled its entire contents. He winced as the acrid liquid stung his throat. He took a deep breath and sighed, feeling the effects slowly playing with him. Still, wine or not, he was firm.

"Yep. And that's bullshit, the whole *'If it can't be seen, it doesn't exist'* theory. Total bullshit." He said without hesitation. He blinked at Lila who simply nodded in silence. She took a long sip of wine, trying to think of what to say next. "And as for other things like ghosts, and, what did you say, poltergeists? I'd love to encounter some kind of apparition. Nothing evil. I always heard stories from my aunts that there were ghosts in houses they grew up in. I don't know." The wine was now making Lila braver than she normally was.

"Okay, what about - what if you saw something here. In our house. What would you do?" Her eyes began to glaze a bit. The wine was working. "I know what you'd do!" She said, eyeing him seductively. Intrigued, Roan leaned toward her, his chin in his hand. He grinned at her.

"What would I do?" He cocked his head to the side. He watched as Lila licked her wine stained lips. "Go on, what would I do?"

Lila bit her lip then continued. "I know exactly what you'd do. You'd grab your camera, and try to capture it. You know you would. "'Roan's Paranormal Activity." She said, slurring slightly. She poured herself more wine. "And then you'd have your proof. You'd show the world what was finally caught on film." Roan laughed but shook his head. "Yes you would." Still, he pursed his lips together;

"You're right; I'd grab my camera. But, I would never, ever try to prove it." Before he could continue, Lila argued.

"Why not? You were all upset about trying to get me to believe you saw a UFO not one hour ago." Roan frowned.

"I wasn't trying to convince you. I was simply stating to you what happened. You're the one that kept telling me that you believed me!" Lila recoiled at these words. "I think you've had enough to drink for tonight." He got up and put the wine back in the kitchen. As he came toward her, she grabbed her glass and downed the rest of it, glaring at him.

"I don't recall asking you if I had," she snapped back. "Why wouldn't you prove it? Why wouldn't you want to show the world that you had living – or not living – proof of some alien being or some ghost or apparition in your own house?" Lila yelled a bit too loudly. Roan was finished.

"I'm going to bed. You're drunk. Let me help you to bed." Lila's mouth opened at his response and she flinched away from him, angry.

"So what if I'm drunk? Whatever. Go to bed. I was just trying to have a conversation." As hard as she fought them, tears welled up in her eyes. Sighing, Roan stopped, his head dropping. Sighing in defeat, he raised his head and turned around. He approached her softly.

"I know you were. And I'm glad we discussed it, and I'd like to continue this discussion, but not tonight. We both have had too much wine and honestly, I'd like to spend the remainder of the evening with you instead of arguing. Now, come on, Honey. Let's get ready for bed, okay? Let me lock up, and I'll be right there. Okay?" He looked at her as she pouted. He kissed her forehead and her arms flew around his neck.

"I'm sorry. I'm stupid. I'm so sorry. I'm drunk and I'm stupid." Sniffling, she let him lead her to the bed.

"You're not stupid. Drunk, yes. Not stupid." He helped her to sit on the edge of their bed. He ripped a tissue out of the tissue box and handed it to her. She blew her nose as he rubbed her back. "Thank you," she said, through the tissue. He stood up and then took it away, tossing it into the trashcan.

"I'll be right back. Let me close the blinds and lock up. Has Hitch been fed?" He asked when the cat rubbed against his leg. Lila's mouth fell open.

"Oh, my God." She closed her eyes. Roan sighed.

"I'll feed him." He left her and walked out into the hallway. He stood there a few moments, rubbing his temples. A headache was coming on. He made the rounds, locking up and securing the house. He fed Hitch, then brushed his teeth, flossed and rinsed. By the time he got back into the bedroom, Lila was lying on her stomach, mouth open, spit oozing onto a puddle on her hand that rested her head, snoring and still in her clothes.

***

"I don't like seeing her like that, Drake. It scares me." Nyx backed away from the tiny hole she and the other two were looking through. Days ago, quite by accident, Alva stumbled past a hole in the wall up near a large beam that overlooked a corner of the living room. All three of them looked through it now, from time to time. "Only to be used as a study tool, not to spy with." Most of the time, that was adhered to. Tonight was definitely a lesson in Human over-indulgence.

"I'm glad that never happens to us," Alva said sadly. Drake flew behind her, landing with a plop on the dirty floor. He carried herbs to a small table where they prepared them to hang and dry. Tying sprigs of thyme together, he nodded at bottles on the nearby shelf.

"Nyx, there is some nice clover honey and some ginger root. Make some tea for her. She'll need it when she wakes up." Nyx took them to their new little kitchen area.

When Roan had moved in after the wedding, Nyx had to stay put behind the wall. After days of pacing and boredom, she decided to start fixing up the shelter to better suit her and the others' needs, just in case. They worked hard making their space welcoming and warmer. Soon the walls were insulated with bits of dried grass and hay. Since there were no windows and the only bit of light that came in was from sunlight that would pour in through a tiny hole in a beam (where Lila had removed a hanging photo, leaving a rather large hole through a stud), Drake fashioned a frame made from grape vines around it. It was lovely! Nyx helped him build a shelf to hang just under the tiny hole, also made from the same vines. It also served as a cute swing to sit on and peer through. The hole was high enough to be forgotten about by Lila and most like never noticed by Roan. This window into the living room was their only connection with the house. From here, they could see the area right in front of the fireplace.

They also created beds and little "rooms" to put them in. They only time they did not spend together as a group was when they slept. They decorated their tiny rooms (actually just divisions in the flooring by planks of wood) to their own liking. Drake loved brocades and chintz. He had a passion for pillows and rich jewel tones. Alva liked chintz too, but was much more conservative. Flowers were her passion and drying flowers were hanging from anything that would hold them.

Nyx loved her color. Green made up her bed in satin. She loved the slinky feel of it. She too loved pillows, but she also had a real love of wood. She loved building and carving. Her little bed was surrounded by an elaborately carved head and foot board, which she had carved in the hours spent alone keeping her presence hidden whenever Roan was around. She rubbed it weekly with sweet almond oil.

Alva braided rugs for everyone, and Nyx helped her braid the largest one for their little common area. Scraps of Drake's fabrics melded quite nicely together. Thin reeds were woven in to strengthen it. The kitchen was very simple, compiled of sticks and pieces of strewn wood that were found on the floor and throughout the area they were in. Lots of great stuff to create a tiny home. It was now a warm and cozy nook for them to live in, at least temporarily. For now, it was perfect. Night was the time that the three of them would leave their shelter in search for food and supplies, herbs and water, and actually go outside.

The loud voices had begun shortly after their supper. The trio flew up to their swing to watch but could not see anyone, just a shadow now and then. Still, they stayed there and listened. By the time they could finally see them, Lila was very drunk and unstable. They flew back down into the common area after seeing the lights go out. Drake brought a tray with honey sugar cookies and honey bush vanilla tea to the table in the center of the room. They each had their own cushion (thanks to Drake), and took to them. The room was warm with a thick vanilla essence. Drake poured and finally said,

"Well. Wasn't that lovely?" crossing his fat little legs. Alva frowned at him. "But, it may just mean that you are this much closer to your goal, Nyx. He does believe in the unexplained." He winked at Nyx and bit into a cookie. Shaking her head, she added cautiously,

"Yeah, but that doesn't mean he likes it."

Drake responded immediately. "Doesn't matter, Nyxie. He can hate it, but the belief is there – once it's planted, it can't ever be removed. It's a part of him. He *knows* it, too. You can't just turn beliefs off like a light switch." Nyx nodded and brushed crumbs off of her cushion.

"Yeah, I know, but now I'm afraid, after hearing all of that, that he'll question not Lila's sanity, but his own. You know?" She sipped her tea.

Alva added, "Not only that, Nyxie, but Lila could resent you for that. I – I don't like this, anymore," she said, her little bottom lip quivering. Nyx had not considered this. Suddenly, she felt her own tears dropping onto her lap. She looked at Alva, who was now sobbing into her tiny hands.

"What do I do now?" She flew away from the table, tears and what looked to be black soot drifted and splashed behind her. When Nyx was sad, black dust followed her (red when she was angry). She crawled into her tiny bed and pulled the blanket over her head and cried into her satin pillow.

Nyx awoke with a jolt. A distant, low roar meant it was raining. She listened, pulling the tiny blanket tightly around her. It felt damp. It was musty and moist inside when it rained, even though it was sheltered. She lay awake, thinking about the conversation with the others. She heard the floorboards squeaking and then a beam of light lit up the ceiling. She threw off her blanket and tiptoed out of her room. Sure enough, a line of dim light lit up the bottom of the baseboard. That told her that someone was awake and walking around. She flew up to the little window and looked into the living room just in time to see the bottom of Lila's bathrobe float out of sight. Lila was in the kitchen. She longed to just fly out of the shelter and into the kitchen. She flew back down to the baseboard and slowly poked just enough of her tiny head through to see around the corner. She then saw Lila walk back toward the bedroom. She heard the bedsprings and knew she had gotten back into bed. She retreated and went to their little kitchen. She ate a few cookie crumbs and then went back to her own bed, snuggling inside the warm blanket. Listening to the roar of the pounding rain, she fell back to sleep.

Lila lay awake. She still felt a bit tipsy but not nearly as much as a few hours earlier. She knew keeping hydrated was the key to avoiding a nasty hangover, so she sipped water. She listened to the rain. It was a heavy rain. It sounded like pennies hitting the roof. She tried to recall the conversation with Roan. It came in flashes. She was sorry she had gotten so drunk. She'd talk to him again. Sober. She turned onto her side. Roan was also sleeping on his side. She moved closer to his body, and slid her hand up inside his pajama sleeve. Roan had told her after they first began sleeping together that he loved when she did that. It told him that all was right with the world. He let out a mumbled moan and moved his body back toward hers to make contact. He smacked his lips, contented. She inhaled and rubbed his bare shoulder. The sound of fat droplets hitting the roof lulled her back to sleep.

She felt a kiss on her head. Lila let out an irritated moan. "Sorry, Babe. I'm heading out," Roan whispered. Lila squeezed her eyes shut, but turned toward him. She opened her eyes, blinking at the bright morning sunlight. She looked up at him. "Gotta go," He said, zipping up his jacket. Lila sat up, yawning and nodding. Roan walked away. Lila got up.

"Hey wait," she said sleepily. Roan stopped and turned to face her. She looked up at him, his six foot two frame towering over her five foot frame. "I'm sorry. I'm sorry I got drunk last night and I'm sorry I was an idiot." Her lower lip stuck out like a child's. Her head hung against his chest. He bent down and kissed her head, then hugged her tightly. Her arms wrapped around his waist beneath the leather jacket. They held each other silently. "I'll make a nice supper and we can talk later." She sniffed. Roan lifted her chin, kissing her lips.

"Now that sounds nice. I love you ... and you're not an idiot," he said, looking into her eyes, red with sleep and too much wine. "I'll call you in a bit." He started to walk away, but then stopped. "Oh. I have decided to have a talk with that kid. Might let him do a re-write. Bye." Lila smiled.

***

Coffee and Ibuprofen seemed to be the special of the morning. Lila's head was pounding. She put coffee on to brew then showered. She dressed and put her hair up into a towel. Going into the kitchen, she smelled something sweet. There on the counter, was a steaming cup. She smiled, looking around.

"Ginger root and honey; the hangover cure. Better than coffee. Drink up!" She looked up and around, finally seeing two tiny legs dangling on top of the refrigerator. "We'll clean up here later." She flew down and landed on Lila's shoulder, just like an obedient parakeet. She kissed Lila's cheek. "There's a lemon poppy seed muffin on the table; let's eat. I'm starving." They sat in the kitchen; Lila in her chair and Nyx sitting on the table, picking bits of muffin. Soon the headache ebbed and before the tea was even cold, she felt normal. Better than normal. Fantastic!

"You're amazing, Nyx. Thank you." Nyx nodded, sipping her tea.

"You're very welcome. We never understand why Humans get drunk, only to feel so bad the next day," she said, shrugging.

Lila replied, "Well, it is fun. A bit of a buzz is nice. I think most people don't realize that when you drink like that, you pee so much of it out, you become dehydrated; that's where the pounding head and wicked nausea come in. Now, if they had their own Fae friend to make potions like this," she held her empty cup up, "everyone would be raging alcoholics." Nyx looked at her. "Okay, I really don't drink that much. I used to, but I just don't like it all that much anymore." She popped the last crumbs of the muffin into her mouth. They sat quietly. Then,

"Today, I'd like for you to finally meet Drake and Alva. Would you like that?" Lila brightened up.

"Of course I would! When?" Naturally, Lila began looking for them. "Where?"

"They are busy this morning, but I thought we could have a nice lunch in your bedroom. I – I mean – we can't take any chances right now. It'd be bad enough for me to be seen, but for the others, it would be extremely perilous." Lila completely understood. She thought for a moment. She'd promised Roan a nice supper. She'd need time for that and some cleaning. A look of worry alerted Nyx. "Don't worry about supper. If you allow us, we can help out with that. Just this once though. While I will always be here for you – and Roan – the other's won't. But I'm sure they'll want to help out. They're very excited about meeting you! Let me tell them to plan for lunch. Can we meet in your room at say, eleven thirty?" Lila nodded, excitedly.

"It's a date. I'll have it all fixed up. What you would you like to eat?" Lila asked, taking the wet towel off of her head.

"You needn't worry yourself. We have everything under control." Nyx flew up in front of Lila's face, her wings fluttering, allowing her to float. She crossed her arms. Smiling, she added, "I'm so happy about this. But, this meeting is very important for all of us, Lila. We will be discussing some of our concerns with you. I trust you have some concerns that you would like to share?" She nodded toward the framed wedding photo on the mantle." Lila sighed and nodded.

"Well, it'll be discussed. Don't worry; this will all work out. We need to do just that; work. That's all."

The first thing Lila did was clean the bedroom. Not that it really needed it, but since they would all be sitting on her bed, she wanted it to be inviting. Never in her life did she ever think that she would go out of her way to make her bed inviting for anyone except her lover or husband; if someone had told her that one day she'd be doing this, preparing her bed for a luncheon with three faeries, she'd think they were crazy.

She changed the sheets and pulled out a fresh comforter. She threw the comforter into the dryer to refresh it and fluff it up a bit. She vacuumed and dusted. It was a warm day, in the upper fifties, so she opened the bedroom window to air it out. Looking around, she smiled satisfactorily. She looked at the clock. Only nine-forty. The phone rang. Roan. It was brief, but just a "'how are you'" kind of call. Roan asked her what she had planned to make for supper.

"I'm not sure. I'm still thinking about that," she mused. He told her he'd see her around the usual time.

27

Lila changed into a soft pair of yoga pants and a long fluffy sweater. Her long, curly hair braided and shiny. She felt like she was going on a first date! It was ridiculous! She didn't really know how to behave. How does one act before meeting Faeries? There was no protocol. As if she was reading her mind, Nyx appeared on her shoulder. Lila let out a squeak of surprise. Nyx giggled, then said,

"Just be yourself! That's what attracted me to you in the first place." Another kiss on the cheek. Then Nyx frowned. "Does that bother you? My kissing you?" Lila raised her hand to her shoulder. Nyx hopped onto it. Lila slowly brought her hand out in front of her.

"Don't be silly! Of course not! Friends kiss all the time. It means a lot to me." She smiled sweetly at Nyx. "I look at it this way; I must be pretty special if a Faerie wants to kiss me. And I'd kiss you back, but I'm afraid I'd hurt you!" Nyx grinned.

"You're absolutely right. Fae don't kiss Humans unless they feel safe and loved by their Human."

***

Lila sat cross legged on her bed. She sighed. She felt too stiff. She unlocked her legs and stretched them out, turning onto her side and holding her head up with her hand. Too casual. As she sat up and brought her legs back up to cross, Nyx flew into the room. She hovered at the entrance. Even in the bright sunlight, she suddenly saw a deep magenta glow approach. Followed by a bright purple glow. Suddenly, two tiny Fae flew in and hovered next to Nyx. Lila found herself sitting up slowly, her mouth opening in curious awe. For a split second, she felt as if she was dreaming. She whispered, "Holy... this can't be happening." Drake flew ahead of the others now and stopped in front of Lila's bent knee. He landed just next to it, taking a deep breath.

"Of course it's happening! I'm here as plain as the nose on my fat face!" Drake added, joyfully. Lila happily shook her head.

"I know. I just – "She was cut short by Nyx.

"Come, Alva. Don't be afraid! She's very kind. Lila, Alva is a little nervous," Nyx said, as she gently took Alva's hand and guided her, in air, to the bed and to Lila. Lila laughed and added,

"Alva, you're not the only one who is a bit nervous." She said, honestly. "Please. Come." She said, gently. As the two landed, Drake stood. Lila looked him over. She had to stifle a laugh. Her eyes sparkled as she took in his face. His skin was almost a periwinkle blue, but his clothing was a deep pink; his vest was a darker pink with gold threads in the seams. Glittering threads

136

throughout. Even his tiny boots were pink. His black hair was spiked every which way, meticulously. His eyes were a deep blue. He was chubby, but it suited him. He was a hair taller than Nyx. He stood in front of her. He ceremoniously cleared his throat.

"My dear lady. I am Drake, a Water Faerie." He bowed as far as his belly would allow. "I come from a land far away, as do the other two. While there are many kinds or species of Water Fae, I am a Sidhe, pronounced 'Shee', which simply means that I live near water; no, I don't live *in* it, and thank the Heavens; ruin this? Please; I think not!" He turned, pointing to his clothing. Lila smiled widely,

"Sidhe. That sounds Irish?" Drake nodded.

"Indeed, Lass! Nyx and Alva are pixies. Their roots come from the Isle of Arran the largest island in the Firth of Clyde, Scotland. My family originates from the tiny town of Valentia, the most western point of Ireland. I was brought up to wear the colors of my origin." His lips pursed and his thick brows knit into a sneer. He leaned and whispered, but loud enough for all to hear, "I hate green on me. Makes me look dreadfully sick." Alva giggled. Drake winked. Lila bowed her head to him.

"It's wonderful to make your acquaintance, sir. Welcome to my home." She said sincerely. After a moment, there was an awkward stretch of silence. Nyx knew that Alva would be next to introduce herself. She gently cleared her throat; she nudged Alva. Alva looked at Nyx, then at Lila and blushed, and felt her face burn. Lila took her off the hook.

"Alva; a lovely name! Welcome to my home." She nodded to her, coaxing her forward.

"Y-Yes ma'am. I am Alva. I am so happy to finally meet you. I have been wanting to meet you for some time now. We, Drake and I, have been trying to tell – to teach, Nyx what she needs to know. You know, so she can safely live here. I think she's learned a lot. I just hope it works out. I have reservations," she offered, bravely. This time it was Drake that nudged her. Lila felt sorry that Alva had already been nudged twice, and smiled at her, encouraging her to continue. "Well, I do. Still, I would like to get to know you better. I think we all need to talk about things." Drake pulled her aside.

"Yes, well I'm sure Lila understands that." He took her aside, Alva frowning even more. "What's wrong with you!?" He snarled at her. Alva violently took her arm back from him. Lila spoke up.

"Drake! That was rude! Please, Alva. Don't be shy. Tell me what you have to say. I want to hear it, it's okay. We all have fears and concerns, here. Come back." She held out her finger toward her in a gesture of peace. Nyx smiled as Lila nodded. "Please." Alva took Lila's finger and allowed herself be led back in front of her. Confidence returned and she began again.

"Let me start over," she said, taking a deep breath. "I am Alva, and I am a pixie. I am standing on this bed with the two most important things in my life; my friends, Drake and Nyx. I care very deeply for them; they are my family. I only want what is best for them. Nyx is in danger now; and actually, all three of us are. I want her to be happy, but her safety is what I am concerned about. She is happy with you." As her tiny voice began to quaver, Drake mumbled something nobody could make out. She continued, "I like you, at least I want to like you. We have to think of our safety, though. We have had many late night discussions about you and your lover. He is now our main concern," She looked down. "I just want Nyxie to be happy." Nyx's brows knit into a frown.

"That's enough." Drake said, standing as tall as he could in front of Alva. "Look, all four of us know this is not something that will happen overnight. I am certainly willing to take as much time as is necessary to ensure that this is something that can happen and keep everyone healthy and happy. Lila, I do have new concerns that I wish to discuss with you, and with my friends. But first, I'm famished. Can we *please* eat?"

The meal was a quiet one, save for a phone call from Roan. Lila got up and opened the blinds. The sky was a periwinkle blue, and that meant one thing; snow was on the way. She shivered, returning to her bed. Alva spoke first.

"Lila, not that we were eavesdropping, but all three of us heard your discussion with Roan last night. All of it." Drake nodded, sadly. He opened his mouth to speak but Alva continued. "I think," she said in a voice that told Drake to hush, "that Nyxie is afraid that Roan might not be able to handle another so-called 'encounter' with the unknown. I have a sneaking suspicion that you agree with her. We all feel this, Lila. What are your thoughts?" Lila tore a corner off of her napkin and played with it, rolling it into a ball.

"The exact same thing you three are thinking." She sighed. "But, I know him. I think he'd not only handle it, but handle it well. It will just take time getting him there. I mean, I think that once he got used to the idea of a faerie living in the house and befriending us, he'd be okay." The longer she said those words out loud, the sillier it sounded. They all laughed. "Seriously, though. I just need to do this slowly. I don't want to scare him and I don't want to fuck with his sanity, either. Sorry, I mean I don't want to mess with his sanity. I know him. He's pretty open-minded about things like this. It just takes him time to get there. I'm repeating myself, aren't I?" Drake finally had a chance to speak.

"I get it. If this is done right, you won't have a thing to worry about; Roan will accept the idea of Nyxie being a friend to you two. Lila –" But before he could continue, Alva interrupted.

"Here is what I fear the most; I am afraid that Roan will not be able to accept Nyxie. He'll have doubts about his own sanity, lose it, and then Lila will blame Nyx for Roan's inability to accept it; their union, marriage, is ruined. That's a very good possibility!" She was sobbing now. Nobody spoke. It was as if Lila had been slapped. It stung. "What if Roan can't handle it? What would you do? What would become of Nyx?" Now Lila cried.

"I don't know! That would never happen! I could never hate Nyx!" she cried. Drake flew onto her shoulder. His tiny chubby hand patted her cheek.

"But Roan is your husband, Lila," he said, softly. "Your soul mate. You were brought together by God. You must stand by him, first and foremost." Finally, Nyx stood up and spoke.

"Look, all of you. This doesn't have to happen in one day. Or a month. A year, even. Let's do this one day at a time. It can't be rushed. Yes, for Lila and me, things happened quickly, because it was meant to be that way. That is our way. I did not find myself here in this house by mistake alone. Something drew me to you, Lila. You know that, and you two know it. You were just open to accepting me. That's neither good nor bad. It happened. Now. I say we stop for today. No more discussion. We all need rest. It's been an emotional day, and quite frankly, I'm exhausted. Lila, my

friend, I thank you for your hospitality. We'll meet again, soon."
She flew near Lila's face. She kissed her nose. Drake kissed her
cheek. Alva simply smiled at Lila and nodded, thanking her. In a
rainbow-like flash, they were gone. Lila stared down at the glittery
confetti on her bed wondering what to do next.

Part Three

There's a weapon
That we must use
In our defense
Silence

When you look at them
Look right through them
That's when they'll disappear
That's when we'll be feared

28

Lila watched through the picture window as Roan shoveled the driveway. Eight inches of snow fell overnight and another twelve inches was expected by tomorrow night. She put another log on the fire and went into the kitchen and checked on the roast. The entire house smelled of warm cider and roasted beef. She motioned for him to come inside. He'd been at it for over an hour, and it was now obvious that he was fighting a losing battle. He saw her and motioned the other side of the car. He'd do that and then come inside. That gave her time.

She ran into the hallway, her thickly socked feet sliding on the polished hardwoods. She quickly knocked on the baseboard, *tap, tap-tap-tap*. As fast as she ran into the hall, she ran back out. She slid her boots on and her coat, hat and gloves. She'd go help Roan.

"Let's go! Hurry!" Nyxie said to the two other Fae. "Hurry!"

***

Roan and Lila both kicked the snow off of their boots against the bricks of the house. Lila smiled. Roan, on the other hand, was shivering. They came inside and removed their coats and layers of clothing. Both put their wet boots by the fire to dry. Roan warmed his hands, rubbing them together. Lila giggled. Roan looked adorable in his grey long johns. She handed him a steaming mug of hot cider. He took it and inhaled deeply. He sipped. "Ah, that is so good." He sipped again, not wanting to leave the spot by the fire.

"I have a surprise for you. Go into the bathroom." He looked at her quizzically. "Go on! Take the mug with you." She watched as he went toward the bathroom.

When Roan stepped into the bathroom, the room was dim, but not in total darkness. The room was lit by candles. Thick towels on the shelf. The tub was filled with water and bubbles. A thermos of cider and one mug sat on the antique stool next to it. The air was warm and smelled of mild pine. He smiled, taking in the scent. He undressed and slid into the inviting water, sinking into it. He could see outside through the skylight above the tub. It was snowing like crazy and yet he never felt so warm in all of his life. A feeling of comfort like he had never felt before came over him. Almost like being in the womb. *Almost.* He closed his eyes, savoring everything from the feel of the bubbles, to the warm hugs of the water, to the clean scent of pine. Real pine, not that awful pine scented cleaning crap or fake pine scent that came in a spray.

"Nice, huh?" Lila said, opening the bathroom door a bit and peeking in. Roan smiled, eyes still closed.

"Mmm hmm. Thank you." he said in a sigh.

"Mind if I join you?" Lila said as Roan's eyes opened. Lila now stood naked in front of the tub. Roan slid up and made room for her. She stepped into the hot water and sat, her back to him. Their bodies squeaked on the bottom of the tub. He wrapped his arms around her, and kissed her soapy shoulder. "I don't ever want to get out," she cooed.

He took the sponge from the edge of the tub and submerged it, then bringing it out, he squeezed soapy water onto Lila's shoulder, then onto her knees. He poured some bath gel onto the sponge and squeezed. Gently, he scrubbed her exposed knees. "I could do this every night," Roan said, nuzzling Lila's ear. His deep voice sent sparks throughout her body.

"Promise?" she replied. Her eyes closed and she relaxed. Her eyes opened when the sponge left her body. She watched as he soaked the sponge again. This time, he traveled up and squeezed water onto her nipple. Lila bit her lip. Roan threw the sponge across the tub. His hands cupped her breasts, his thumbs circling her nipples. She felt him harden behind her. She drew in air and held her breath, only to let her breath escape in a long moan. He kneaded her flesh then let his hands roam down to her belly beneath the water. Instinctively, her knees fell apart. He kissed her neck then kissed her ear. His tongue darted out and licked the lobe. She moaned loudly. Her body started moving against his. His breath in her ear made her crazy. His hands reached around her thighs and pulled her by her legs closer to him. His hands slid down until he was touching her coarse hair. His fingers raked through it, making her breathing quicken. Lila moved her body against his, making the water slosh out of the tub and splash onto the floor. He teased her, playing with her hair, pulling it. Lila bit

147

her lip. Finally, his thumb found her most sensitive spot and she cried out. He massaged her, slow delicious circles. Every now and then he'd stop and thrust his finger deep inside her body. She tried to reach behind her to grab him, but the sensations were just too much for her. He rubbed her and slid his fingers deep inside her as he kissed her neck. Her leg fell over the side of the tub, and her body slid so that her head could rest on his chest. His lips found hers and instantly her tongue found his and he sucked on it. She'd pay him back, later. Right now, all she could do was to give in to what he was doing to her. His fingers now fucked her hard as his now wrinkled thumb teased her even more. He could feel her wetness even in the water and he spread it over her, slow then furious, and then slow again.

Finally, she could take no more and held his hand in place until she climaxed with a scream as more water spilled out of the tub. It was the most intense orgasm she had ever experienced. She turned and kissed him deeply. She cupped him and scratched him. He moaned out loud. She smiled, licking her lips. "Your turn, my love."

***

Sitting in the kitchen, Roan and Lila sipped coffee. Wild winds blew outside. The morning was a deep blue outside. Lights from other houses glowed in hues of yellow and orange. The radio played softly in the background. The regular jazz program that they both loved listening to was interrupted for updates on road closures, and the long list of school closings. Lila buttered her toast and let out a frustrated sigh.

"I have no idea why they don't just list the places that are open. I mean, it has taken them twenty- two minutes to go through the list. Just tell us what's open for Christ's sake!" Roan nodded.

"Well, then they'd have nothing to do, my love." he said, reading the latest headline on his laptop. Lila disagreed.

"Sure they would. They could play the music they normally play." She took an exaggerated bite of toast. Roan eyed her over the laptop.

"You alright? You seem a bit tense. I thought you'd feel a bit nicer after last night's activities," he said with a growl in his voice. Lila eyed him back. She felt herself get wet. She blinked and searched for something to say. She shrugged instead. *How does he do that?* she pondered silently. *Just his voice can melt me like ice cream on hot pavement.* She swallowed her toast and grinned.

"That was all your fault. All I wanted to do was take a bath," she teased. Roan balled up his napkin and threw it at her playfully, hitting her on her mouth. "Hey!" She threw it back. It hit him on the shoulder and then fell onto the floor where Hitch batted it with a paw and then chased it into the living room. "Yeah, that was fun. Let's do that more often." She got up and hugged him. He pulled her into his lap and closed the laptop.

"You got it. Right now, though, I need to find out if teachers are off or not. I'm sure we'll get administrative leave. I'm not an 'essential employee,' he said, sticking out his lower lip. Lila kissed his cheek, scratching her mouth. She then ran a finger across his growing beard.

"Oh, you're essential, all right," she said, giggling. Still, Roan looked outside, eyebrows knit with concern.

"I'm not going anywhere in that crap. And it's supposed to snow all damn day. I'm staying put and so are you." She got up and began rummaging through her pantry. She coughed, her throat suddenly tickling her. A tiny spasm of back pain pricked her. Another cough and it was gone.

"I feel like baking. I could make a pie, or a cake. I could put on a pot of beans. Or -" Roan interjected.

"Rigatoni. That rigatoni you made last winter was so good. We could make some bread to go with it. I like to bake, too." Suddenly, Lila felt really good. She found a box of rigatoni and had everything she would need to make that, a few loaves of bread and a pecan pie. She would even have enough left over to walk some over to Erin. All of a sudden, the day seemed perfect and it wasn't even nine o' clock, yet.

"You know, it's too bad we don't have our tree up. This would be such a sappy, Christmassy kind of day," Roan said, as he stood looking out of the picture window. Snow was falling at an alarming rate, and the winds were just fast enough for the National Weather Service to issue a blizzard warning for the state. "I could go up into the attic and get the lights down. I could at least get those up. What do you think, Lila? Lila?" He walked into the kitchen. She was on the landline.

"So, what are you going to do then? Sit there all alone? Just come over. Bring something to sleep in. Bring what you want, but just get over here, Erin." She hung up. She looked at Roan who suddenly looked annoyed. "Oh, come on, Babe. Look, Patrick is stuck in San Francisco. The airport is closed, Roan. She's over there all alone." She looked at him. He sighed.

"I know, I know. You did the right thing. It's fine. Maybe we can dust off a board game or find the deck of cards." Lila snickered, kneading dough.

"No strip poker."

29

"It's s-so cold.' Nyx said, shivering. The smells wafting in from the main house made them all wish they could just come out for a moment. They heard music. Christmas music. The sounds of laughter and dishes clanging. Suddenly they were stopped by another sound. The squeak of nails against wood being removed. A moment of panic overtook them all. They flew in the direction of the noise. Around the corner it was at its loudest and the three watched as a square piece of wood fell inward to the main house. Peering into this new opening, they saw a huge face appear. Lila. A collective sigh of relief was hushed by her.

"Shh! Here; a few blankets. I wish I could let you build a fire. These should keep you warm. This is the opening to my bedroom closet. I'll leave it open for a bit so that you can get some warm air. If you find yourselves getting too cold, come in here. Just be careful. I don't expect that Roan will need anything from in here. If he does, I'll get it. Gotta go!" The trio took the blankets and decided to just go into the closet. It was so cold behind the walls. Now they would be safe and warm. For now. Drake eyed the doll house.

"It's just too small. If it were just a wee bit bigger, it'd make a grand home for us!" An idea was planted and he grinned. "Just wait until this storm is over!" He let out a loud, - "whoo-hoo!"'- and was instantly hushed by Nyxie and Alva. They huddled together, pulling flannel shirts tightly around them, and giggled quietly and gleefully like kids having a slumber party.

***

"I'm glad you went with all blue, Roan. It's absolutely beautiful," Erin said, using her bread to sop up sauce from her plate. Tiny blue lights now outlined every window on the bottom floor of the house. All the lights were out except for the blue ones and together with the roaring fire, it cast a calming hue in the room.

"There; my secret's out; I love decorating for Christmas. I *am* Clark Griswold, reincarnate." The three of them spent the evening discussing everything from the weather (which was getting worse) to days of Christmases past. The power began flickering around eleven-fifteen and though they had a generator, Roan decided that he would stay by the fire and keep it going while Lila and Erin took the master bed. While Erin washed up (by candlelight, of course), Lila quickly checked on the trio in her closet. She coughed to let them know she was there, but that made her cough more. Finally she swallowed and opened the closet door. She knelt down. "Psst! Everyone still here? Are you okay?" she whispered loudly.

"Warm and snug!" Alva said through a yawn, though she was anything but warm. Lila informed them of the power outage and gave them some extra actual blankets and helped them to line the walls. "I'm going to have to seal this back up for tonight. It's okay; Roan is going to sleep in the living room. But my neighbor and I will be sleeping in here. Snuggle up, there's no telling when the power will come back on."

The trio had never been so scared in all of their lives. They were not used to such frigid temperatures. Still, the closet was warming up and they felt safe now, knowing that Lila was just outside the door. Still, they huddled close and prepared for sleep.

The next morning was bright. Very bright. Thick white snow covered everything. Trees were heavy with it, bending dangerously close to their snapping points. Cars were hidden, with an occasional rear-view mirror peeking out or antennae poking out of the deep snow. The sun was blinding. Still, it warmed the house and as she approached Roan in the living room, she opened the drapes, letting warm sunlight heat the chilly room. The power was still out, but already neighbors began the strenuous task of digging out. Lila went to the attic and pulled out the old coffee urn she had and made a bunch of cocoa and set it on the porch with a collection of mugs and cups. This was the one thing that she loved about snow; it brought everyone out and together. Erin hugged Roan and Lila goodbye and told them to keep calling the power company. They begged her to stay, but she insisted on getting things in order at her own house next door. If she needed anything, she knew where to come.

Seeing as it was a Friday, Roan took his time digging out the car. He did manage to shovel the steps and sidewalk off. He brought the empty urn inside. "That was a hit. I think you've made some new friends, Lila." He looked around. He couldn't find her. He finally went into the bedroom. She was asleep. He gently closed the door and went about washing all of the mugs.

When suppertime came around, he had the leftover rigatoni warming on the stove. He had to wake Lila. He hated to wake her, but he knew she'd get upset if he let her sleep. He shook her gently. She stirred and coughed. She sat up slowly. She grimaced.

"I think I overdid it shoveling. My chest and shoulders hurt." She took a deep breath. "God, Roan, that hurts. Damn, you don't think I cracked a rib, or something? It feels weird." Roan tucked her in.

"Stay in bed. You overdid it, Lila. I knew this was going to happen. Let me get you some ibuprofen. Want some tea?" She nodded.

"Blueberry. Thank you." She tried to sit up, but it hurt. She winced as she propped herself up against three pillows. That helped. "I don't need this now, Roan," she croaked. Minutes later, he returned with a tray with tea, a glass of water and two ibuprofen pills. He sat with her as she swallowed them.

"How long have you felt like this?" He asked, taking the glass. He fluffed her pillows. She knit her eyebrows together in thought.

"Actually a few days. A week. I thought I was catching another cold. I dunno. I feel icky. I'm about to start too." He nodded, knowing what she meant. She purposely stuck out her lower lip. Roan kissed it.

"Want the heating pad?" She nodded. He headed for the closet. Lila sat up.

"Wait! It's in the bathroom!" Roan turned around. "It's under the sink." He shut the closet door.

"Okay, okay. No need to yell!" He left for the bathroom. Lila threw the covers off and bolted to the closet. She opened the door, gave the trio a warning glance and pulled the heating pad off of the top shelf. She quickly nodded and then shut the door. Wincing, she touched her upper chest. She climbed into bed.

"I got it. I'm sorry, it was under the bed." She heard the bathroom door shut and Roan's footsteps coming back. "Roan, could you plug it in for me?" Her ebbing fear and relief that the trio was not found made her forget how hard she was breathing. Roan plugged in the pad and sat again on the bed.

"Babe, I don't like the way you sound. Can you breathe alright?" he asked, now very worried. He watched her gasping.

"Yeah, I'm just, I got winded looking for the heating pad." Roan eyed her suspiciously.

"You said it was under the bed," he said, exasperated. Breathing a bit easier, Lila answered.

"It was. On your side," she lied. She sipped tea and then put the heating pad on her lower belly. "That's much better. Thanks, Baby," she said, smiling. Thinking that a bit of food would be nice, she asked Roan to fix her a plate when he was ready to eat. "Bring a tray in here; we can eat together. Come on; it'll be cozy." Roan headed out. She could hear his slippered feet shuffling the floor. She then put the cup down and squeezed her eyes tightly shut. Whatever this was in her chest, it hurt like hell.

Lila hardly ate. She tried hard to conceal her pain. It worked for a while but Roan eventually noticed how uncomfortable she was.

He put his arm around her and massaged her shoulder. It felt so good. Soon she fell into a restless sleep.

***

Nyx awoke with a start. Something was not right. She looked around and found Drake and Alva snoring away. It was very quiet except for the low volume of the television in the bedroom. Someone was selling some ridiculously low-priced pan set. Still, something was wrong. She climbed out of the flannel shirts and over the mountain of boxes. If she had flown, her wings would have illuminated the room and she knew not to take that chance so she climbed. She jumped onto a sweater and crawled down its sleeve. She could jump if she could just open her wings like a parachute and not actually fly. It worked. She was now at the base of the door. She could slide out from under it with room to spare. All she wanted was to make sure that Lila was okay.

She lay on her belly and slid her body through the opening. She looked around and saw Hitch. His back was to her, but he was awake and licking his paw. She heard an odd sound. Breathing, but like snoring, only it wasn't snoring. It sounded labored. She quickly ran to the hope chest that was at the foot of their bed. She grabbed the comforter and very slowly began climbing. All she needed was to see Lila. When she finally saw her, she almost screamed. She knew instantly that Lila was ill again, very ill. She looked around frantically. She saw the tea cup on Roan's side of the bed on his nightstand. She crawled under the bed and came out at his side. She took a deep breath and taking every chance her instincts told her to ignore, she flew up and knocked the cup onto the hardwood floor, smashing it. Immediately, the cat spun around but Nyx was already crawling out from under the bed by the closet and her little body slid under the door just as Roan sat up.

"What the hell," but before he could look down, he heard Lila. Her breathing was very labored. He shook her. While her eyes opened, she seemed to be completely out of it. "Oh, my God ... Lila?!" Grabbing his cell phone, he dialed 911.

30

It took the ambulance two hours to get to their house. All Roan could do was to keep Lila upright. It seemed to not only calm her, but also to help her with her breathing. He now sat beside her bed in the emergency room. Thankfully, it wasn't busy due to all of the snow. Test after test had been run. He told the doctor that she had had pneumonia the summer before. This kind of seemed like the same thing, only without the fever and chills. He played with a Styrofoam cup, pinching it and pulling balls of it off and flinging them. He ran his hands through his hair. He watched Lila sleep. She had oxygen prongs in her nose, a pulse-oximeter on her finger (her oxygen level was dangerously low in the ambulance, 82), a blood pressure cuff on her right arm and an IV in her left. Lila looked so small now. A nurse came in and adjusted her oxygen flow. She smiled sweetly at Roan.

"Sir, would you like some coffee? A sandwich?" He shook his head. "Sir, it's going to be a long day. Let me bring you a tray." He sighed and nodded, thanking her. He watched her as she walked down the brightly lit hall past the nurses' station. He suddenly lost it and began sobbing. He felt so useless and alone. No family to speak of to call. Except her cousin Karen. He made a mental note to call her as soon as he got some news. He tore a tissue from the little box on the table and wiped his eyes. The doctor cleared his throat to note his presence, then pulled back the curtain and entered her cubicle. He quickly turned and left, returning with a beat-up leather chair. He sat and shook Roan's hand.

"Mr. Donovan, I'm Dr. Glenn." Roan nodded. He took a deep breath. The look on the doctor's face scared him. "Well, I'm glad she's here. Your wife is very ill," he said gently. The doctor took out MRI films and held them up to the bright lights. "I'm seeing some areas that are somewhat troubling, here and here. You say she had pneumonia last summer? Bacterial?" he asked Roan. Roan shrugged. He looked at the images and tried to decipher what it was that he was seeing.

"I think it was bacterial. I think they treated it as such. I'm not sure," Roan said, shrugging. The doctor nodded.

"Well, her breathing is very labored. Has she been coughing? Spitting up blood?" Roan stared at the doctor.

"What? No – no blood. She's been coughing, but not that much. She only started complaining tonight. We thought she may have overdone it shoveling snow." He shook his head in disbelief. "What are you saying? Does she have lung cancer or something?" It just came out before he could stop it. The doctor hesitated then nodded.

"We think so, yes; lung cancer." The words slapped him. They were said so casually. No warning. No preparation. They were the last words Roan heard the doctor say. He expected the doctor to laugh that off. *"Oh, don't worry, sir. It's just bronchitis!"* Cancer. He watched the doctor but heard nothing now; lips and hands moved, but nothing else registered. Nothing until,

"Oh. And, she's pregnant," the doctor said cautiously. Roan let out a laugh. The doctor looked at Roan over his glasses. "Sir?"

"That's not funny. I don't know why I'm laughing," he said, angry. The doctor nodded, understanding.

"I know. It's not funny at all. Matter of fact, it's very, very serious. It's about as serious a situation as I have ever seen in my tenure." Both were silent. Both searched for words. Roan still could not quite grasp the idea. "The first thing we need to do is to determine how far along Lila is in the pregnancy." Roan looked at him.

"Tonight, she told me she had cramps. She asked me for a heating pad." He said, looking past the doctor, focusing on nothing. "I don't know when her last period was. It seems like it was a while, though, I guess; I don't keep up with that," he said, embarrassed.

"We can try a transvaginal ultrasound. That should give us a ballpark idea. In the meantime, we need to do a lung biopsy." Roan fell apart. Again, he tried to hear and understand what the doctor was telling him. All he knew was that what should have been the most blessed day of their lives was now the scariest.

***

Lila watched the doctor leave her hospital room. Roan took her hand and kissed it. The oxygen prongs were seriously annoying her now. She put on a smile.

"Well, that's that. No treatments for a while," she said gently. Seeing the look on Roan's face she let her smile fade. "Roan, it's not all 'doom and gloom' you know." Not wanting to hear any of this, he stood and went to the window, looking out into the snowy parking lot of the hospital.

"Not all 'doom and gloom.' How can you say that? I'm sorry; I didn't mean that. I just don't think this is a good time to have a baby, Lila." He turned to her. "You know? If under any other circumstances." Lila sipped her water then replied.

"I know what you're saying. I can't do that, Roan. I won't." Without hesitation, Roan was back at her side and again he took her hand. Tears welled in Lila's eyes and spilled down her face. Roan thought for a moment and chose his words carefully.

"Lila, let's get you better. You heard what the doctors said. A stage one cancer. Bronchial Carcinoid. Let's kick its ass! Surgery is a good possibility, and along with radiation and chemo, you have a good chance of beating this. We can always have another child, Lila." She vehemently shook her head.

"I can't do that. I cannot do that, Roan. Do not ask me to abort this child, because I won't. You heard the doctor. Let's wait. We can consider those options after the first trimester. If it was a stage two, then I might have other considerations, but as it stands right now Roan, I – we – are having a baby." He stared at her incredulously. His emotions were exposed and his voice broke down.

"And that cancer will just grow and fester more in that time! Baby, I just want you to get better. That is the only thing I care about, the only thing!" Lila tugged her hand out of his and yelled at him.

"Don't you care anything about your child? How can you say that to me!?" Both were crying now. Beyond words, Lila sobbed. Roan watched her. He knew that no matter what he said to her, no matter how he felt about the situation, she would be the decision maker in this. Still, he wished she could see his side.

"We can have another child, Lila!" Roan yelled at her, then lowered his voice. "You have to focus on your health! You have to fight for yourself, now. Your body isn't strong enough to carry a child." his voice cracking, he choked back a sob.

"And what if we can't? Huh? What if I never get pregnant again? I would have aborted the child for you. Not for me, for you. And I'd resent you for the rest of our lives, Roan. I want a child. I'm having a – our child! Let's talk to another doctor. Please? If another doctor agrees with you, then I will consider it. I don't think any doctor would tell me it's okay to have a baby if they didn't honestly think that I could do it. Roan, I'd have the abortion if it meant my life. I have choices. It won't be easy, but the other two said I could do this. I can start treatment at thirteen weeks." She began coughing and Roan stared at her. He nodded at her.

"I'd rather have you resent me for the rest of our lives than to have you die on me, Lila Jean." That made her cry all over again. "But I'll agree to speak to another doctor. Let's get a third opinion."

31

"Nyxie, Lila needs you now more than ever. So does Roan. We need to come up with a plan. It's either now or never; Roan must know about you. They both need you now." Nyx had read about the cancer in the pamphlets left in the kitchen while Roan was busy at the hospital. "No tea can fix cancer," she said, weeping. Still there were things that could be done. For now, she asked Drake and Alva to basically move in and stay for the duration. Duration of what? The disease killing her? The pregnancy? "Just stay with me. With us. Lila needs Roan and she needs me. I need you," she begged, although that wasn't necessary; they agreed.

***

Lila lay on her bed. It felt so good to be home. No more gross smells and sounds of the hospital. The first thing she did upon arriving home was take a long, hot bath. No Fae magic, this time. She scrubbed her body until it was red and all of the hospital stink was gone. She then stood in a hot shower, shampooed and conditioned her hair. Then she cried her eyes out. She washed her face and said aloud, "No more tears. I've washed them away and now it's time to kick some cancerous ass." She then got out, dried and put on some sweats. Her favorite Nordic socks kept her feet warm.

She read some of the literature the third doctor had given her about carrying a healthy pregnancy to term while fighting all kinds of different stages and types of cancers. The third doctor was very much in favor of her having this baby. She was very matter of fact about it and Roan, while still very worried, now felt a bit better about becoming a father. A bit. He still had reservations.

Nyx and the others heard her cries of anguish. They decided that the very next time Lila was alone, it was time to meet with her. Roan must be made aware of them. He needed them, and yet he had no idea just how much he would come to rely on them.

The streets were still horrible, but Roan had to get groceries for the house and promised Erin he'd pick up some for her as well. They decided not to tell anyone about Lila's diagnosis (either one) for a while yet. As far as anyone knew, Lila was just not feeling well. Lila went to the bathroom. She was nauseated. Sometimes she did forget that she was actually pregnant. She got sick and though she felt horrible, it was reassuring that she was still able to feel the normal symptoms of pregnancy. She came back into the bedroom to find the trio sitting on her bed and a steaming cup of tea on the night stand. While the three knew she was ill, that's all they knew. Lila smiled at them.

"It's so good to see you guys! The tea smells good. Is it safe?" They looked at each other. Alva shrugged.

"Safe for what, Darling?" Drake asked.

"Safe for the baby, of course," she said, grinning. The three of them looked puzzled. Alva spoke up, worried as usual.

"We thought you –" She hesitated. Lila understood and helped Alva out of her questioning.

"I am, Sweetheart; I have cancer. Lung cancer. And I'm pregnant. Nice, huh?" The trio searched for words. Lila eyed them sternly, yet she smiled.

"It's okay. We're thrilled," she lied. "Now, is the tea safe for a pregnant woman?"

The four of them discussed the new situation. They all agreed that it was imperative for Roan to not only see the trio, but to accept them as soon as possible. Lila suggested that she have a long talk with Roan tonight. They all agreed. "I have to say, I'm pretty damn scared." They all concurred. "This could make or break us."

32

The house was perfumed with the scent of rosemary and chicken. She closed the oven door and reset the timer. She turned on the burner to start the potatoes boiling. She stretched, raising her arms up high over her head. She rotated her shoulders. They ached. Her eyes scanned the little table in the kitchen. Usually a potted aloe plant and a bottle of vitamins occupied it.

Today two inhalers and seven prescription bottles littered it. Only one bottle was for the pregnancy, the prenatal vitamins. The rest were for the symptoms of lung cancer. Three were pain medications. She didn't feel she really needed these. At least, not yet. She let her arms fall and she sat at the table. She knew that life as she had known was now and forever changed. Even the way she handled normal everyday tasks was weird. She could do them, but now Roan wanted to do everything for her. He now treated her like a fragile china doll. She hated it. She was trying to let him help her, but it only infuriated her. Finally, when she mentioned vacuuming the living room and seeing Roan get up to do it, she lost it. She screamed at him. *God-dammit! Will you stop it, Roan!* Whether or not she was really just upset that he could not let her do a task so mundane as vacuuming or finally letting out the frustrations of her situation, she let him have it. She screamed at him, using words that she thought could never leave her mouth. She hit him, balling up her fists and hitting his arms, his back. She shoved him hard away from her. By the time she was finished, she was coughing badly and sobbing. Roan simply stood there and let her hit him. He let her get it all out of her system, even if it meant letting her use him as a target. He knew she had to let her feelings out. He just happened to be in the line of fire. She collapsed against him and for the first time, he felt how truly weak her body was. That rage took every ounce of energy out of her. He let her cry and heard her sincere apology. He nodded, kissing her. She let him lead her to the couch where he stroked her head until she fell asleep.

What Lila didn't see was Roan heading to the bathroom and falling apart. He undressed and turned on the shower and cried his heart out. He let the hot water clean his body while his tears cleansed his soul. He knew she was right about some things; she wanted to just live as normal a life as she could, while she could. He would just have to fight the urge to run to do things for her. She would ask if she needed or wanted help.

Lila thought about how she would begin the strange conversation that would introduce him to the trio. All thoughts of cancer and pregnancy were now pushed aside as she tried to gather words that would make it sound as if she was not under the influence of drugs or losing her mind. The more she tried to put a sentence together, the harder it became. No matter how she rearranged the words, it still sounded ridiculous. She twirled her hair in her fingers. *I'm just going to have to do it. Just say the words.* She told herself. After supper. No wine. Straight talk. She straightened up, coughed then smiled. "God help me," she said toward the Heavens.

Part Four

I'll tell you about the magic
It'll free your soul,
but it's like trying to tell a stranger 'bout rock n roll.

33

"There is nothing like a roasted chicken. Lila, this was fantastic. Did you get enough?" Roan asked gently. He felt the need to tread carefully. "Want some more?" Lila shook her head.

"Oh, no. I'm stuffed! I'm saving room for pie. The kid suggested some pecan pie. I had to listen." She smiled, patting her still-flat belly. She too seemed to be stepping lightly. She wanted to include their child in conversations like a normal couple expecting a baby would. Still, the words stung him, mocking him. She ignored his eyes. She knew he resented this baby, and she hoped and prayed that after tonight, after finally bringing him into the world she had been hiding from him for all of these months, he would no longer view his child as the enemy. And that if he chose to be a bit open minded, things could change for the better, for everyone. She picked up her fork. She licked it clean and then shined it with her napkin.

"You have an open mind." Roan eyed her over his glasses, across from her. "I mean, well, you're pretty open to new stuff."

His eyebrows knit upward. A sourness filled her throat. Her words were not working, and she felt stupid.

"I'm not following you," he said, tilting his head, smiling sweetly. "What do you mean?" She squirmed in her chair. She twirled the fork in her hand and held it up, as if she were inspecting it for spots.

"Just what I said." Laying the fork onto the table she went out of her way to make sure it lay perfectly straight then she looked at him. "I mean, you aren't so skeptical of stuff, after what you experienced with the UFO. You are open to things that can't be explained." Roan nodded, but his expression changed from understanding to confusion.

"Stuff. What stuff?"

"Like Bigfoot roaming the hills or Nessie in the loch in Scotland?"

"Uh, no. I think that stuff is way over-emphasized," he replied, still eyeing her.

"That's not what I mean. Well, okay; I get that ..." She was getting angry at herself.

"Sure, people see these *things*, but I don't believe it's truly Bigfoot or the Loch Ness Monster," he said, scooping up the last of his mashed potatoes. Lila nodded.

"Why not?" Before Roan could answer, she shook her head and began again. "What about other things? Are you open to the thought of, say, seeing a ghost?" she asked, shyly. Roan grinned then swallowed.

"A ghost? I've never seen one," he said, laughing. Lila tilted her head.

"That's not what I asked you. I asked if you were open to the thought of seeing one. What if you did? Or, what if you saw something so amazing that you just could not wrap your head around it? Would you dispel it? Or, would you want to try to see it again? Maybe even invoke it?" She stopped herself. She knew she sounded silly. Roan let out a confused laugh and simply stared at his wife.

"Did you see a ghost?" he asked her. Lila blinked rapidly. "What's this all about, Lila?" He wasn't taking her seriously and it irritated her.

"No, no. But, seriously; what would you do if you saw a something in this house?" She picked up a cold asparagus stalk and shoved it into her mouth. "Something you couldn't believe you saw." Roan crossed his arms in front of his chest.

"Didn't we do this, already? What's going on? Have you seen something, here in this house? You did see something!" Lila bit her lip as Roan's concerned eyes bore through her from across the table. "Tell me what's on your mind, Lila." The tone of his voice told her she had to stop playing with words. She could feel his irritation building. Not only that, but she began to see a bit of doubt on his face.

He thinks I'm losing it, already, she thought. She decided to try a different tactic.

"You never answered the question." She instantly regretted the tone she used. She went for it. "Roan, something has been going on here for the past few months." Throwing it out there, she waited for him to react.

Nothing.

He sat there, expressionless. "I didn't tell you because, just like you do now, you would have thought I was nuts and probably would have had me locked up." Roan could stand no more and though he tried to keep his cool, he was losing the battle.

"What the hell are you talking about, Lila? Are you cheating on me?" Roan asked, a tinge of hurt coating his anger. All of the color left her face. She felt faint. *Where the hell did that come from?!* she thought. Roan pushed the chair away from the table and knelt at her side. "Dammit, Lila! What's going on?" His voice shook her, and his eyes were sharp and angry. Her face flushed and she felt bile rise in her throat, burning her. How dare he accuse of her of cheating on him. Like she had time to! Anger rose like the bile and she fought to keep her cool. Still, she had never considered that angle. She stood and pushed him away. Her eyes, as angry as his, fought with him.

Before anyone could say another word, a sudden flash of greenish-gold flew across the dining room. A trail of emerald gathered on the hardwood floor and across the dining room table. At first, Roan did nothing. He simply blinked. Lila's anger now ebbed away and tried to hide her growing grin, but soon her smile was just as bright as the dust on the table. Roan's eyes grew.

"What the hell was that?" He turned and looked in the direction of the flash. He looked back at Lila. "What was that!?" For the first time, Lila saw a great fear in Roan's eyes. A real skin-crawling fear. He was shaking. She stood and took his hand.

"It's okay, Sweetie. Come with me. Come on." He pulled his hand away, his face losing color.

"No. Oh, hell no." Roan started walking backwards, toward the kitchen. "I don't know what the fuck is going on, but leave me out

of it. I don't want any part of whatever the hell is happening here."
Lila followed him. She approached him slowly and took his hand
again. She hated this; he feared her, now.

"Roan. Look at me. Please!" she said, sternly. He looked at her,
but only for a second. He looked anxiously around the room. Lila
put her hands onto his face, cupping his chin. "I need for you to
come with me. Listen to me! If there was anytime in my life that I
need you to do as I ask, now is that time. Don't be afraid. Trust me.
Remember our marriage vows and trust me. I will not harm you,
nor would I ever do so. I will never let anything harm you. Now.
Please Roan. Come with me. Do this for me and our child." He
looked at her incredulously, shaking his head. "Please Roan. I'm
begging you; don't be afraid. Don't be afraid of me. I love you." His
breathing was almost as labored as Lila's now. "Take my hand.
Now, come with me." Lila held out her hand. Fear still took over
Roan, but he slid his hand into hers, letting her guide him. For the
second time in his life, he felt totally out of control, but he let Lila
lead him. "Come on." She tugged at his hand. He turned and began
walking with her, allowing her to take him. She led him back
through the dining room and into the living room. Green fiery
flecks still sparkled on the floor. Roan looked down at them.
Puzzled, he looked to Lila again. She smiled gently then nodded
ahead. He suddenly realized that they were following this path.
But to where?

"Please, Lila. This is really scaring me now." Lila stopped in
front of the potted Ficus tree. She squeezed his hand.

"It's okay. I promise. I love you so much, Roan. I've hated
having to hide things from you." He looked at her again,
dejectedly.

"I knew it. I knew you were hiding something from me. Who is it?" His voice cracked. Now Lila took his face into her hands.

"Please listen very carefully to me. It is not what you think it is. After tonight, I'll never have to hide a thing from you, ever again. Don't be scared. This is a good thing, Roan." She leaned over and kissed his cheek, lingering. "Now very carefully, look into the tree." She smiled at him, pointing with her left hand.

Roan shook his head.

"No." Still, he squeezed Lila's hand. He looked at the tree. He squinted then cocked his head to the left. He shrugged.

"I don't see anything. What am I looking for?" he asked. *He wasn't trying*, Lila thought. She totally understood that, too. *Does he want to find anything? If he doesn't see it, does he think it won't exist?*

"Look again. Come on, Baby. It's okay; I promise." Again, she motioned toward the tree. He let go of her hand. She felt as if he was really letting her go. She didn't know why, but she suddenly felt very small and alone. She bit her lip hard and tasted salty blood. She wanted to see his life change. She hoped and silently prayed that it would change for the good and that he would accept what he saw. She watched his eyes darting. Turning on a lamp would have helped him see much faster, but the thrill of the search suddenly filled her and she knew he'd eventually see. He continued looking and seemed finally eager to find something. He was about to take a step to the right when he stopped. He stood motionless. He leaned in closer to the tree. Blinking, he tried to focus. His arm rose and his hand moved toward a leaf. He used his index finger to move it. He stared for a moment.

"What is that? I think I see something." Lila leaned in to look. He had found it. He just didn't know what he was actually seeing yet. "I think – is that a doll?" He turned his head toward Lila. She said nothing. She watched as he looked again. She too looked, as she wanted to see exactly what Roan was seeing. "Lila, what is this? It's a doll! It's just a doll!' He laughed. "That's what you wanted me to see?" He chuckled through his words. She smiled as he stared.

"Keep watching, Love," she whispered to him. This time, she grasped his hand. "Now, I'll remind you to keep our wedding vows in mind." He looked quizzically at her. With every ounce of courage she had, she simply said, "Nyx, this is my Roan." She squeezed his hand tightly and watched his face as he looked into the tree. A soft green light began to appear around the tiny figure in the tree. It sparkled and then the shape of wings began to appear, flowing softly like hair beneath the sea, iridescent and fragile. He squinted again, trying to see better. Soon the light was at its brightest and Roan was staring, unable to look away. Suddenly, a wee voice said,

"Hello, Roan. I'm so happy to finally meet you." Roan instantly dropped Lila's hand and backed quickly away from the tree.

"Oh, shit. Lila, what is that?" Roan croaked in a low, terrified scowl. "I mean it. What is that?" Lila looked at Nyx and shrugged. Now Lila was scared. Scared that Roan might not handle this well after all.

"Not *what*. Who." Nyx added. She stood and slowly walked to the end of the branch, her wings folding behind her. Her shimmery body illuminated by the blue Christmas lights. She stood at the end of the branch with her hands on her hips. "Well?

Aren't you going to introduce yourself? It's okay; I won't bite." Roan felt the room spin and nearly fell. Lila had to quickly run to his side and help him to keep from falling.

"What the – what the hell is going on? How are you doing this? Who are you? What are you?" he cried. "This isn't happening. I can't do this. I can't!" Lila pulled him to the sofa and sat next to him. The fun was over. Now it was time to tell him the truth.

"Roan, when you went to Ireland to bury your brother, I was sick, remember? I started seeing things. Things I could not understand. Things I wasn't sure I could ever understand, let alone tell you about with you thinking I was crazy! What you're feeling now, that's how I felt!" She let her words sink in. She wanted him to say it out loud. "What do you think you're seeing, Baby?" She brushed his long hair out of his gorgeous but fearful eyes. "Say it." His head was in his hands now. He quickly looked up and yelled.

"A faerie! A fucking faerie!" As soon as he said this, Nyx flew. She flew high to the ceiling and then down toward him. Roan flinched, stumbling backward. Lila grabbed his arm and pulled. He stood again, but shielded his eyes. Nyx hovered before the two of them. Green dust wafted like snow to the floor. Lila leaned over and ran her finger through it and brought it to Roan.

"Pixie dust! Real pixie dust!" Nyx said, and giggled, then covered her mouth. Roan let his hands fall to his sides and looked at her finger. Lila took his hand and gently opened it, then rubbed her finger and thumb together, making dust fall into Roan's hand. He touched it. It then disappeared. He shook his head. Lila quickly continued.

"When I was sick, I kept waking up to find things. Weird things like my dirty cup in the sink was not only clean, but put away. A dirty sinkful of dishes done when I know nobody did them. Then the tea. I'd wake up to hot tea. I didn't make it. After a while, I thought there was actually a burglar in the house, but then I knew no burglar makes his victims tea, or lays out clean pajamas for his victims before he robs them! She finally showed herself to me. I probably reacted close to the same way you are right now." Nyx laughed

"She told me she had a gun and would shoot me," Nyx said, matter-of-factly. Lila stifled a giggle and smiled at her.

"She is my faerie. She found me by accident." Roan couldn't take anymore.

"I need some air. I gotta get out of here for a while. Shit, I can't leave you, Lila! Please, just an hour. I need to take a walk and try to understand – I need to clear my head," He ran to the coat tree, grabbed his coat and mumbling something neither could understand, he zipped up his coat and walked out into the snowy night.

***

The night air burned Roan's lungs. White plumes of steam blew by his head as he tried to ease his breathing. His feet crunched the already packed snow. All of this was just too much for him to take. *Cancer. A child. Now this? A fucking faerie!? So this was why she kept talking about all of that paranormal shit. All that talk about UFOs and things we can't control or predict. She was trying to feel me out.* He kept walking. He looked at the houses. Slowly the neighbors were able to put their Christmas lights up. He stood and caught his breath. Never had he felt so badly, and yet so confused. He turned around and walked toward home. *I have an open mind. Now, I just need to learn to trust it.*

***

"It's okay. He'll be okay, Lila. Now, you mustn't cry. Drink this. It will help." She watched as Lila blew her nose. and then sipped the tea. "The worst part of this is over now. He knows; it's done. Now, we can move forward. Lila, I know things seem like they will never get better," She instantly regretted her words. "Oh, Lila, I'm sorry. Things will get better. I know they will. We just don't know how, quite yet, that's all. Lila wiped her tears.

"I feel so hopeless. I am sick. I am pregnant, and should be so happy, but how can I be happy when I may not even live to see my child? And now I may have just scared off the only person on this planet that I care about. The damage could be irreversible. I just want my life back to the way it was six months ago." Lila jumped when she heard the door shut. Roan was setting his wet boots by the fireless fireplace. He slowly came into the kitchen where Lila and Nyx were, Nyx sitting on top of the sugar bowl. He stood by the kitchen table. Shoving his hands into his pockets, he opened his mouth to speak. He closed it. He took a deep breath. He stood silent. He looked at Nyx, then at Lila. Blinking, he took another breath.

"I'm sorry, Ma'am. My name is Roan Donovan. I'm scared to meet you, if you must know the truth." Nyx nodded, understanding. He turned to Lila. "I am so sorry. I love you, Lila Jean. I don't know what the hell is happening here, but one thing is certain. I will never leave you again. I love you. You just have to give me a tiny bit of time, which I know is so precious to us now, to get around this. Okay?" He kissed her and her arms flew around his neck. She sobbed. Nyx grinned.

"Ahem. Your tea is getting cold. Drink up!" she said happily. The couple kissed again and then came apart. "Careful, Roan. You'll spill your tea." Lila laughed and Roan pondered.

"Now you know how I felt!"

34

"If meeting one faerie in your life isn't enough to make you question your sanity, how about meeting two more?" Nyx asked Roan. Together, Nyx and Lila introduced Roan to Drake and Alva. To say it had been an emotional day was silly. It was a day of learning, even for Lila. Questions were asked. Myths were dispelled. The main objective was for the trio to get Roan to understand one simple yet important fact: Lila brought this on. Even without her knowing it. Drake stepped forward and took Lila's hand.

"While it's true that Nyx happened to find this house by accident, it was no accident that she found Lila, Roan. You see, Fae only find a Human to care for when it's meant to be. From the moment Lila was born, it was her destiny, and Nyx's, to come together. Most Humans are born with a kind and good disposition. Lila is kind, no? She is fond of Mother Earth; that's easy to see. Just look around. She gives back to her! She is a protector and advocate for her, and she always has been." Nyx flew onto Lila's knee and sat.

Roan, still new to all of this, simply stared. Now and then, he'd shake his head like a dog, trying to make sure he wasn't losing his mind. "Humans who give back to the earth are precious. Nyx has been on a journey to find Lila. It's not easy for us to find our Human. It takes not just random acts of kindness, but a pure kindness that just pours out. No, Lila is far from perfect; no Human is perfect. Fae are not perfect, but sometimes, a Human's soul and passion for good will guide their Fae to them, unbeknownst to them, until they find themselves in a situation or predicament. Nyx found Lila. She may not have known at the time that she was coming to the end of her search, but when she did finally see Lila, she knew she was home." Everyone was silent for a while. Roan let this sink in, yet he was still having a very hard time with the reality of it.

"So, what about me? Do I have a Faerie of my own?" He asked, sarcastically. The words hung for a bit longer than Roan thought was appropriate. "Guess that answers my question."

Alva stood and said, "You never know, Roan. You might. It's impossible to tell. Seeing a Fae is rare in itself. To actually meet and befriend one is, like Drake said, only seen when a Human is destined. You may be. Chances are, however, you are not. Still, you are a part of Lila's family, and while Nyx is here for her, she will, if you let her, become a part of your family. An extension, if you will. She will always care for Lila, both emotionally and physically." This time Roan stood. He ran his hands through his hair.

"She's sick. You know that, right?" His voice cracked. "She is very sick. She's carrying my baby. Can you save her?" The words came out without his even thinking. "What can you do?"

Nyx cleared her throat. "Yes, we know. Lila is a very strong woman, Roan. Her state of mind is a big portion of how she recovers, and if. Lila, you've been touched by a Fae, meaning that one – three – have been drawn to you. You've been kissed by a Fae, as well. Fae kisses are very powerful – and very rare. For a Fae to want to kiss a Human, that person is finer than the finest diamond. Roan, you can wish for it. Ask me, and I may grant you a healing wish. Keep in mind, though, that healing does not always happen overnight, although it sometimes does. And can seem quite miraculous. So-called 'spontaneous healings' have been known in medical science to happen more than you might think they do. Still, I am no magician; I can't just blink and make her cancer go away. I wish I could. But circumstances are different here. All we can do is try, but you must choose your words very, very carefully, Roan; Lila." Now Lila was confused.

"Wait. Are you telling me you can possibly grant me a wish? But that it might not come true?" The trio nodded and in unison replied,

"Yes." Roan and Lila eyed each other. Both were beyond being able to comprehend this. Drake flew onto the coffee table.

"A healing wish, though, can often just lead you to those people or circumstances that can best help you with your condition, in the way best for you. I believe you call it ESP or refined intuition. It is a natural state, actually, yet so many Humans have lost that part of themselves. As it is developed more, the possibility of Seeing and Hearing beyond the five senses increases. Those who have been kissed by Fae do find this to be easier." His voice lowered into a whisper. "You've been kissed, and quite often, Lila. Fae don't kiss for pleasure. We kiss as a seal of understanding. When you are kissed by a Faerie, it's to show you that we have our full trust in you, and that we are not afraid of you. If Fae have any reservations about a Human, they'll never kiss them. So you see, you are able to see. You may not have to ask for Nyx to grant you a wish; you may now have the power to see what you need in order to survive. Still, that may take time, and time is not your ally. It may take you far away from here. Again, that is probably not in your best interests right now." Lila felt her head spinning. She held up her hand.

"I need a break. I need to go lie down. I'm sorry." She left the room. Roan went after her. He was getting angry but didn't want to further upset Lila. He helped her into bed. He gave her some water and kissed her. He ran his fingers through her hair and she was asleep within seconds. Roan closed the bedroom door behind him. Entering the living room, he saw that it was empty, but heard sounds coming from the kitchen. A warm aroma of sweet leeks and mushrooms filled the room. On the table a bowl of soup was waiting for him. He stood by the table, as if waiting to be invited to sit in his own kitchen.

"Have some soup. It's Lila's favorite," Nyx said sweetly. Roan sat and looked at the soup.

"Couldn't have made me a big steak, huh?" he mused. Nyx walked toward him across the table.

"We don't eat or prepare the flesh of animals. We have a very close relationship with all creatures and therefore never eat them. We do, however, use their milk. We love cheeses and sweet butter is our favorite. Butter on freshly baked bread is the best thing in the world." Roan reached forward for the glass of water and knocked his spoon onto the floor with a loud CLANG. He bent down to get it and when he sat up, a plate with two hot pieces of buttered bread was now next to his soup bowl. It was a darker brown bread and had what looked to be sand on it. His mouth opened. "It's honey-dust bread with the sweetest butter you'll ever have." It smelled divine. Roan inhaled and felt like he was being hugged and comforted. He tentatively picked up a piece. He tasted it and the moment it touched his tongue, he knew she was right; this was easily the most delicious bread and butter he could ever remember having. His eyes closed as he savored the morsels of bread. "Try the soup." Now Roan was not a big fan of mushrooms. Still, he wasn't one to shy away from tasting new things, especially if they are made by Fae that make a something as simple as bread and butter taste amazing. He sipped from his spoon. Again, flavors danced and he smiled.

"Wow. I could get used to this." He smiled. "Thank you," he said in all seriousness. He looked at each Faerie. Each nodded to him, smiling. It was the first true moment of friendship between Roan and Nyx. Drake and Alva looked on approvingly. The first hurdle was cleared. Now, the real work would begin.

Part Five

Sweet visions attend thy sleep,
Fondest, dearest to me.
While others their revels keep,
I will watch over thee.

35

It amazed Lila just how quickly life started to return to a somewhat normal routine. Roan was back to teaching. She went back to her classes when felt up to going, but she knew she'd have to give them up soon. There were moments when she felt just awful, and soon school was simply out of the question. She began seeing an obstetric oncologist. She was now entering her thirteenth week, and the topic of today's visit would be her options for beginning treatments. Her doctor explained that the drugs used in treating her kind of cancer were still being evaluated and that she could be taking a risk, even after the second trimester, of hurting her baby. Without even thinking about it, she refused them.

"If you choose not to do the chemo and wait until your baby is born, there is a good chance that it would be too late." She might live another six months to a year, the doctor added, looking at Roan. Lila was adamant. Roan, however, was still very upset that

Lila would not undergo the treatments. "But again, we'll just have to keep monitoring everything. Let's take it a few weeks at a time. Right now, things have not changed. The films show no new growth or spread of tumors. Now, let's check this baby."

Her belly was just beginning to show a familiar lump. "Have you felt it move, yet?" Lila shook her head. In all honestly, she had forgotten about this. "You will soon. Now, do you want to know the sex of your baby?" The couple looked puzzled. "It's ultrasound time. I want to have a good look, check the placenta and see how things are progressing. We can tell the sex at this age." Lila took Roan's hand. He seemed a bit distant. The doctor noted his response. She put the transducer down. She took off her glasses. "Mr. Donovan? Is there a problem?" He shook his head in silence. "How do you feel about this baby, Mr. Donovan?" The question threw him and Lila. He was silent. As much as he tried to fight them, tears welled in his eyes, spilling out. He tried to speak.

"I – I just..." He sat down and put his head into his hands. Lila was shocked. She looked at the doctor, hoping to come up with the words to say something, anything, but she couldn't gather them. She was at a total loss for words. The doctor walked around the exam table where Lila lay waiting. She put her hand onto his shoulder. Roan sobbed. For the first time, he truly cried his heart out and didn't care who saw him. "I'm s-sorry. I just can't do this. I don't want to lose my wife. I can't lose you, Lila! I feel like that baby is stealing you away from me! I can't lose you. I can't," he sniffed. The doctor handed him a box of tissues. Taking one he buried his face in it. His cries stabbed Lila so sharply that she too was openly weeping. She sat up, using the paper on the exam table she was lying on to wipe off the conducer gel off and she jumped off of the table. Not caring that she was still naked from the waist down, she knelt in front of her husband and wrapped her arms around his shaking body. His head fell with a hard slap against her neck and he kissed her as he cried. He buried his lips into her neck. The doctor left and closed the door. "I'm sorry. I'm so sorry, Lila." He lifted his head and looked into her eyes.

Lila's heart broke. This was the man she loved more than anything on this earth and seeing him like this- eyes blood-red, brimming with fear and hopelessness, his mouth unable to contain the spasms of crying – she brushed his tears away with her thumbs and kissed his forehead hard, squeezing her eyes tightly closed. And yet, even after seeing all of this; witnessing this man falling apart in front of her, she still could not think about ending her pregnancy. First of all, it was too late. Or was it? She didn't know. She tried to speak. Her words were clouded by her own sobs.

"Roan, I know. I know. You must understand; it's not the baby that's killing me, Roan. It's the cancer. And if we do things right, we might just do this. Do you hear me? You know what I'm talking about." She gave him a look that offered hope. Like a mother nudging her nervous child on his first day of Kindergarten. "We can do this. This is you and me and our child!" She took his hand and held it to her belly. He pulled it away.

"No, don't! I don't want to," he pleaded with her. "Don't make me." Lila stood, angry.

"Don't make you what? Love it? Don't you want to love it?"

"I'm afraid to love it! I'm afraid to," he sobbed. Still, Lila yelled.

"How can you be afraid? It's you and me! We created this child, with love. I know what you're saying. Blame the cancer!"

"I'm afraid to love it because if I do, I'll fight for it and I'll lose you. I'll lose you! I am so afraid!" There was a soft knock on the door. The door opened and the doctor stepped inside. After Roan and Lila settled down, she spoke softly.

"I won't pretend to understand what you two are going through right now. I honestly don't know how I would handle a situation like this. But, it's like we said earlier, a week at a time. Mr. Donovan, I must do this test. Now, if you don't wish to know the sex, I can leave that out. You don't even have to stay for the exam, although I highly recommend that you do. No matter what, this is your child, sir." Lila looked at Roan.

"Please, Roan. Stay with me. I need you; we need you. Let's find out what we're having. Please?" He blew his nose. He was still visibly upset.

"Forgive me, Doctor Ellis. I —" Roan nodded. He didn't have to finish. The doctor helped Lila back onto the exam table and squirted more cold gel onto Lila's belly. She turned out the lights in the room. She slid the conducer over Lila's skin. She tapped into the computer and did a lot of what she called "'mapping."

"Well, baby looks good, a good size. There are the feet. Hands. There's the umbilical cord." The doctor noted both parents were glued to the screen. Roan took Lila's hand. Tears fell from his eyes again, but this time he was quiet.

"Is that a nose?" Roan asked, pointing. Lila smiled. The doctor nodded.

"Yes. Looks like yours." Roan let out a small cry, followed by a laugh.

"Poor kid," he mused through tears. Lila beamed at her husband. They looked back at the screen, smiling.

The doctor took a few more measurements. "See that? See where it looks like it's blinking?" She looked at them both. They nodded. "Well, that is your daughter's heart beating." An audible gasp arose from the both of them. "Congratulations; it's a girl!" For a brief moment, the cancer was forgotten and finally, joy erupted in the tiny exam room.

I'll make you happy, baby, just wait and see.
For every kiss you give me I'll give you three.
Oh, since the day I saw you
I have been waiting for you.
You know I will adore you 'til eternity.

36

When the trio was told that the baby was a girl, nobody was surprised. "We knew! We can't tell you some things, Roan," Drake giggled. Nyx was a huge help during the next few months. Lila tired very easily and suddenly meals were not made, laundry piled up and dishes "soaked" for a bit too long. Not for long, though. The trio helped whenever they were needed.

Roan was a doting husband, rubbing Lila's feet and shoulders. Her back hurt a lot and he'd rub that when she looked pained. One day, he came home from school with a bag. He gave it to Lila. She smiled and took out a box of crayons and a coloring book, *Faeries and Gnomes.*

"I saw it in the toy section. I couldn't resist," he said, grinning. When Lila began opening the box of crayons, he quickly took them away. "Nope, these are for my daughter." When he took the book and crayons into their bedroom, she suddenly cried. Sometimes he truly did the sweetest gestures.

When Lila entered her sixth month, the cancer began spreading to other nodes in the lung. She became weaker and very tired. While everyone did what they could to ease Lila's pain and suffering, she was tired. Her doctors now made house calls once a week to check on the baby and her oxygen levels. The doctors decided that bed rest was a good idea now and the bedroom was turned into a hospital room. Lila hated it. Still, all the medications she needed were there. Nyx made Lila a soothing tea that eased the pain in her back and shoulders. Soon the teas would not be enough. The trio took Roan aside one sunny afternoon while Lila was sleeping, and discussed the one thing, the one idea that they didn't want to mention to Lila yet that might just save her.

Drake arranged lunch in the living room. He brought cushions out and candles. Nyx made a lovely salad and Alva made cakes and scones. Nyx flew into the room that would soon become a nursery for the baby girl. Roan was smoothing out a wallpaper border. It was also in this room that Roan insisted the trio live. He even made one of those silly "fae doors" that, while most of their friends would think was a charming addition to their garden, actually functioned. The trio had planted all of their herbs and spices just outside this window. The lavender plants concealed the lovely little door.

Roan fully accepted the trio now. Meeting the other two was fascinating for him. He thoroughly enjoyed Drake and Alva. For whatever reason, Alva opened up to Roan. She thought that perhaps, just perhaps, he was her Human. Drake was just entertaining, and wickedly smart. So, after discussing it with Lila, they both asked the trio to live with them forever. Roan did this, in part, to please Lila at first. After all, he'd do anything for her, but he had to admit that while it was totally the craziest thing he'd ever experienced, he loved having them in their lives.

He came out with Nyx and sat in the living room. He sipped hot ginger tea (his favorite). Alva flew onto his knee.

"It's time to talk about some things, Dear. As you know, Lila is getting worse," she said softly. Roan nodded.

"I know. The doctor said that if Lila can carry the baby another ten weeks, the baby will be able to survive." Drakes head fell.

"Roan, that's not what we're talking about. We need to discuss what we can do to help her. We need to talk about something else. Something that might ... scare you." Drake was having a hard time. Alva took over.

"Roan, Lila is dying. You know that. You cannot deny that it is coming close to the end of her life. There is something that we have not told you. Something that might help her to live, but it's not as easy as you might think. It's not like we can just wave pixie dust and say some magical words. It's much more than that, and we are not so sure you are willing to even hear what this option is." Nyx nodded in agreement and continued.

"Like Alva said, Lila is getting weaker, and we don't know when the end is coming. Right now, though, our main goal is to keep her comfortable and happy, we must keep her alive so that she can deliver your daughter. I know that sounds crass, I don't mean for it to. But those are the facts that we have to deal with. Do you agree that we should make her as comfortable as possible?" she asked, looking for any sign of doubt in Roan's eyes. He nodded.

"Yes," he sighed. Drake spoke again.

"Now. I need to again ask you to have an open mind. What we are about to share with you, first of all, cannot ever leave this room. Do not ever speak of it, except to Lila, and only when you fully understand everything we explain to you. Can you promise us that?" Roan's head spun. What more did they expect him to swallow?

"Yeah! I promise," he said, exasperated. There was a long, awkward silence. Nyx finally cleared her throat.

"There is a way to keep Lila alive." She looked at Roan, who's mouth opened, but she waved him quiet. "But it requires full understanding and acceptance not only from Lila, but from you, as well. It will not work if there is even a drop of doubt in your mind or heart. It is irreversible. Once it's done, it's done. There is nothing that will ever be able to reverse it. I know we don't have a lot of time anymore. I will explain this to you, but I must ask that you keep quiet – don't interrupt – and listen to me. Alva and Drake, I know, will help you to understand. I don't want a decision made tonight. I want you to think about it overnight, and don't discuss it with Lila until we speak again.

***

"There is no way that I can do that. No way." Roan shook his head, closing his eyes. He stood, though he seemed lost. He sat again. "I can't do that to her, and I can't do that to our daughter." Alva flew onto his shoulder. She kissed him. It was the first Fae kiss he had ever received and though he knew that she was now truly his protector, and that he was her Human, he still pushed the plan out of his mind. It was just too much for him to comprehend and he felt sick. Alva flew to his knee as he sat. She sat, crossing her legs. Her lavender eyes sparkled.

"Dear Roan, you have been through so many difficult times, and in the past few months you have witnessed things that most Humans never see, or see only in their wildest imaginations. You have been forced to accept things that you still question. But, as sure as I am speaking to you and sitting here, you know these things are real. We only speak of things that are true. We don't stretch truth. We don't lie or deceive. You know that." Her voice was soothing and gentle. "You could call it a miracle if you wanted. Still, with all of that being said, we – at least us three – are not seers of the future. We cannot foretell what will happen tomorrow, in our world, or yours. When Nyx found Lila, she had no idea that one day Lila would become so very ill. And even if she could've foreseen that, nothing would have changed; she would have come. Now, we are at a crucial point in all of our lives. We don't have a lot of time. Consider what we have told you and think about what it truly means for her, and your daughter. As for you, I will always be here with you. Please, Roan."

Lila toweled off and wiped the steam off of the bathroom mirror. She saw dark circles under her eyes. She frowned. *At least I still have my hair*, she thought, running her fingers through it. She inhaled deeply. The steam felt good, but she began coughing. Her coughing had increased dramatically in the past week. She bent over and coughed harder. Wetness dribbled down her chin. When she looked into the mirror, she saw the blood. She touched it and looked at it. Bright red. She took a tissue and wiped it off, throwing it into the wastepaper basket. She'd tell no one. She brushed her teeth and, closing the towel around her, went to the bedroom.

Her favorite pants and sweatshirt were laid out nicely on the bed, her slippers on top of the pants. The drapes and blinds were open as was the window. Cool air wafted in with a tinge of spring warmth. She could smell the grass and the budding lavender. She went to the window and looked out. The Crepe Myrtle that was to the right of her window was just coming into bloom.

She decided to dress and go outside. She'd leave the clothes on her bed for later. She threw on jeans and a Henley. Her hair was still wet, but she combed it out and put it into a ponytail. She patted her round belly. "Come on, baby girl; let's go see how our garden is growing." She coughed and cleared her throat. Her pants were loose, even though they were maternity jeans; her frail body looked lost in them. She made a quick cup of coffee and took it outside with her. She stood by the herb garden. The trio had done such a nice job. Peering, she noted their little door. A roundish triangular shape. It looked like something out of a faerie tale, for sure. All kinds of herbs and flowers were growing; pansies, lilacs, foxglove, peonies and roses. In the herb garden lavender, clover (that grew everywhere, anyway), heather, thyme, rosemary. "Baby girl, this is going to be so pretty come summer."

Her thoughts moved toward summer. Would she even be here? She forced a smile, but tears came. "I don't want to die, baby girl. I want to live and watch you play out here. I want to watch you grow." She poured her coffee out and sat in the old Adirondack chair weeping softly.

Roan looked out of the attic window. He watched Lila cry. He could feel her pain and knew that she was trying so hard to come terms with her fate. She would not be around to watch their daughter grow. He put down the boxes of winter clothes and watched his wife for a long time. He watched as she rubbed her belly. *Already, she's a momma*, he thought. *She's comforting her baby.* It was a bittersweet scene. The sound of wings broke his reverie. It was Nyx. She looked worried.

"Come with me." She flew down out of the attic. He followed her. Nyx quickly flew ahead of Roan. Hovering until he caught up with her, she suddenly darted into the bathroom. Hands on his hips, he caught his breath.

"What's up?" He asked, his breathing slowing. Nyx flew and landed on the rim of the wicker wastepaper basket on the floor. He knelt down. She pointed.

"Blood." Her voice was a whisper, but he heard her. He picked up the tissue. "It's fresh. I take it you did not cut yourself shaving?" She eyed his full, yet trimmed, beard. Slowly, he shook his head.

"No. No, it's hers." He stood up. "Damn." It was coming fast. He tried to keep his composure but his voice faltered. "Okay, Nyx. I've made up my mind. Let's do this. Let's talk to her. Let's do it!" He threw the bloody tissue into the toilet and flushed it, as Nyx flew onto his shoulder. "Let's go get her."

The fire lit up Lila's hair, making it look like spun gold, even though it was dark brown. The night was unexpectedly cold and a fire seemed right. She sat with Roan on the couch, but both were huddled together. Balled up tissues littered the floor and coffee table. The Trio sat on cushions on the coffee table. The idea for the next plan of action had been brought up and, after a few moments of letting it sink in, the group took turns voicing concerns and questions. A lot of tears were shed. Lila finally understood. Still, she had to hear it once more. Blowing her already-swollen nose, she asked Nyx to tell her again.

"We will forget about the doctors. We will keep you comfortable until it is time for you to deliver your daughter. We will begin gathering the necessary items from the garden. We will need your wedding rings. You will feel no pain and neither will your baby. If we can plan things just right, you will live to see your daughter being born. You will hold her. You will be with her until the time comes to leave. We will all be with you, and I will escort you to your new home."

"I can talk to Roan? I can talk to my baby? Will they hear me?" she sniffed, and squeezed Roan's hand tightly. Nyx nodded.

"Of course you can. Just as I am sitting here talking to you, you can do the same." Roan began to weep.

"I want Lila – you – to live. If this is the only way," his head fell. "I will love you for all of my life, Lila Jean. I'll never stop." Lila smiled and touched his cheek.

"I'll love you all the days of my life. My life here, and my life – there. But, I want you to go on, Roan. I want you to love again." Roan got up and walked to the window.

"Never. I can't." Drake spoke up, wiping his tears with the back of his fat hand.

"Lila will love you forever, Roan. Her love will change, though, as will yours. We love differently. After the process is complete, you will love her, but it will be a divine adoration for her, as hers will be for you. That will allow you to, if it's right, fall in love again someday, without ever losing your love for Lila. And for Lila, that would be one of her wishes come true, not only for you, but for her, as well. She will always be your daughter's mother. Whether or not you choose to share that with your new partner is up to you, but know that we are always going to be around, so think carefully before you choose. We cannot – Lila – cannot interfere with this process. Love, in the Human world, is something we Fae can't quite grasp. It's lovely and sweet to see, but we don't love the same way. It's not bad, it's just - different. You will go through an obvious time of grief. Not only is it important for you to experience it, but it is also a diversion from us. Lila will, in the Human sense, have died."

Lila sipped some brandy. It felt warm as it burned her throat. She blinked. "So then what? What does Roan do? What about the doctors?" Drake turned and smiled kindly at her.

"He leaves. He takes the baby and a few items of need and he flees. To Ireland. We will all go, as well. He and your daughter will begin a brand new life. Ireland is not a strange land to Roan. It's my home as well, and Scotland is Nyx's and Alva's homeland. Still, we shall all live together; all of us! Roan has already picked out a house. Old and in the woodlands, outside the town of Portumna in County of Galway. It's lush and green and there are lots of trees and places for a little girl to run and play. She will grow up happy there, Lila. She can play while you are freely with her, and you are free to come and go in the same house. Roan has plans for your house within his house. It's beautiful with every comfort. And Alva and I shall also have a house of our own, yet it will be safely hidden. The gardens will thrive with flowers and herbs. Roan and your daughter will live like royalty."

Roan smiled. He sat back down next to Lila and rubbed her belly. "I'm changing our name. Roan Quinn. The town is small but needs a teacher in the high school. Mr. Quinn, art professor, at your service."

The group was silent. Eventually the Trio went to bed in the room that would never be used as a nursery. Lila and Roan enjoyed a silent interlude before finally deciding to go ahead with the plan. The next few weeks the couple would enjoy each other. They planned their daughter's future and during this time they would become even closer, their love growing stronger by the day. Slowly, though, they began the process of saying goodbye.

And you wonder where we're going
Where's the rhyme and where's the reason
And it's you cannot accept
It is here we must begin
To seek the wisdom of the children
And the graceful way of flowers in the wind

37

The morning was rainy and though it was warm, a chill was in the air. Quite unusual for mid-June. Lila was nearing her ninth month. She was thrilled that she was able to carry her baby this long; however, she was nearing her breaking point. The size of her womb now crushed what was left of her delicate lungs. She seemed to take a sharp turn overnight. She was tired in every sense of the word. Her body was worn out. It was almost time.

Nyx and Alva began gathering herbs. Lavender, sage and clover. Roan collected the rainwater from the glass vial he had rigged up on the porch. He would need a full cup of it. He had that with an ounce to spare. He would also need one drop of placental blood after the baby was born.

Drake went about gathering the items that would complete the potion. An amethyst; Lila's birthstone; an emerald, which was Roan's birthstone, and a perfect little pearl which, of course, would be their daughter's. A piece of Nyx's tunic which happened to be green satin. A cup of Fae Sugar (the same as honey sugar only much finer). After these were gathered and set up in the kitchen, Drake turned to Roan. With a forced smile, he asked for the final two objects; their wedding rings. Roan laughed nervously. Without a word, he led Drake into the bedroom.

When they arrived, they noted immediately that Lila was in pain. When Roan ran to her side to see if she need pain medications, she shook her head furiously.

"It's time. The baby. It's time," she panted, her head rocking back and forth. Panic washed over him. Drake flew out of the room with an audible *zip*, leaving magenta dust in his wake. Roan sat on the bed and asked her how long the contractions had been occurring.

"I don't know, maybe an hour? I thought it was the cancer. Back pain, but I think my water broke too." She winced as another pain began gripping her. Roan pulled the bedclothes off of her body. He saw how thin she was despite being heavy with child. It was alarming. The bed was indeed wet. Lila squirmed. Roan put a folded towel under her bottom. The trio flew in.

Alva quickly flew onto the top of bedside table. "Now, we know you can do this. You have all you need to deliver your daughter. We will be here to aid in any way we can, but this is your show now," she said sweetly to Lila. Roan nodded, but still seemed lost. Drake flew in front of his face and hovered there.

"You can do this, man!" As Roan turned to look at Alva, he noted the table now had scissors and fresh shoe laces. A metal basin and a tiny syringe. Lila let out a loud moan.

"Oh shit, I can't do this! God, help me!" Pain shook Lila's body like an earthquake. The trio flew over to the dresser and sat. Each one offered words of encouragement and praise, and each fanned her with their wings. The contractions intensified and Roan tried his best to get her though each one. No painkillers were available. She had to endure the fiery pain of birth without any kind of relief other than the brief respites between contractions. Breathing was a big part of enduring labor and was a way of getting through each pain. For Lila, however, this simply didn't work. Breathing normally was a challenge. The trio would step in and talk her through each of the contractions, reminding her of how brave she was and that soon it would be over; she'd finally see her beautiful baby girl.

Hours passed. Roan was beyond exhaustion. His body was tired, but it was his mind that was truly taking a beating now. He hated seeing Lila suffering, and even prayed for God to take her, only to then beg him not to; to just let her get through this and live long enough to see her baby. He could tell that she was very close to her breaking point. She fought for every precious breath now, and the strength to cope with the agonizing pain. He gave her sips of water. She slept between contractions, which were coming very close together, now. Roan hated seeing her brief moments of peace sliced by searing pains. To awaken with such force and agony, he could not see her enduring this for much longer. Suddenly, she stopped wincing. Her eyes opened and searched for Roan. "I'm here, darling." Lila sat up. Her legs fell apart. A look of fear came over her sweaty face. Before Roan could react, Nyx flew to the bed.

"It's time. She's pushing now." Remembering what he needed to do, he put on the pair of surgical gloves and climbed onto the bed. Kneeling before her open body, he watched as his daughter slowly emerged down the birth canal. Lila was laughing.

"Oh God, this feels so good. I have to push." Roan laughed with her. Lila's hands grabbed the sides of the mattress. Her face turned a deep shade of red with her efforts to push. She coughed horribly, spitting out disease into a tissue. Roan then saw that the baby's head was about to come through.

"Lila, stop pushing, now. You can't push. Let the baby come naturally," Roan said gently. Lila cried.

"I can't stop! Oh, God, I have to push! Get it out! I have to get it out!" Lila lost control, and Roan then changed his voice.

"Lila, stop! You can push in a few seconds. Stop." The trio flew to her side. They spoke to her gently. They whispered encouragement and soon Lila was screaming. "This is the worst part, Baby! You've got this! Fine; scream. Scream loud!" Lila howled. Roan stared as his daughter's head finally emerged. Lila let out a long gasp. She coughed violently, spitting into another tissue. Angry red blood dribbled from the corner of her mouth. "Okay, Lila. Push! Give it all you have, Baby. Push!" Lila bore down and grabbed her thighs, bringing them up to her body, opening herself for her daughter. "That's it! Keep going! You can do this! Oh, Baby, you're doing it!" As Lila let out one final scream, her daughter slid out of her body and into her father's hands. She laughed, but her coughing was keeping her from seeing her baby. With one hand, Roan handed the glass of water to her, which she drank quickly.

He looked at his child and while he wept tears of joy, he noted that Lila's breathing had changed. It was now quiet and shallow. He quickly tied off the umbilical cord and cut it in between the two pieces of shoelace. He then handed the baby to his wife. Her arms engulfed her squirming child and her eyes opened. She looked down at her red, angry daughter, smiling. She cleared her throat and kissed her daughter, still wet with the soup of birth.

"Juniper. Juniper. I love you so much." She looked at Roan. "Juniper? I don't think it's Irish." She breathed. "Our Juniper Pearl." Roan laughed.

"Juniper Pearl Quinn; welcome to the world." He kissed his daughter and then his wife. It was then that he noticed that Lila's eyes were closed and that her breathing had become very slow. Dread filled him like boiling water. Drake spoke.

"It's starting, Roan. Wrap the baby and then take her wedding ring. Take them into the kitchen. The afterbirth is coming. Hurry." Roan quickly cleaned off and wrapped Juniper and put her on the bed. He took off Lila's wedding band and then his own. He ran into the kitchen and placed them onto the counter next to the other objects. He ran into the room.

"Now, when the placenta comes, place it into the metal basin," Drake instructed. It didn't take long and slid out effortlessly. He lifted it and put it into the bowl. "Now, take the syringe and insert the needle into the vein, not the red arteries." Roan looked up at Drake, confused and panic-stricken. "The blue one is the vein. Draw up half a syringe full. Cap the needle, and take it into the kitchen. Leave the kitchen and come be with your family." Drake waited until Roan returned. There was a basin of water now sitting on the dresser with fresh blankets and a tiny diaper. "Wash Juniper and diaper her. Bring her to her mother. Do not leave her. We will return with the potion. She'll be okay now. We have time."

Roan approached his wife. She was awake again. Her thin fingers smoothed Juniper's downy hair. He kissed Lila again.

"Let me clean her up and I'll bring her back." Lila nodded. Roan took the baby to the dresser and unwrapped her. He dipped a soft sponge into the warm water and bathed his daughter, who simply looked around. Her tiny lips pursed as he wiped her body clean. She yawned and let Roan diaper and swaddle her. He brought her back to Lila. He carefully helped his daughter into Lila's arms.

"You did it, Baby." He kissed her. Her thin hand touched his cheek.

"We did it. And, already you're the perfect father. You're so good with her. She knows it, too; she's not even crying," she said, her voice a frail whisper. She finally got a really good look at their child. Dark auburn hair and, of course, blue eyes. "I hope they turn green," Lila said, inspecting her baby. As frail as Lila was, she brought Juniper to her chest and began nursing her. Roan was certain that this wasn't possible but soon the sweet smacking sounds of nursing filled the room. Lila gasped then giggled. "Feels weird, and kind of hurts, but in a good way." Roan took a photo of them.

"Perfect." He snapped a few more then began cleaning the soiled linens. Lila was able to move to the other side of the bed while Roan changed the sheets. He even brought in new pillows for her. He gently cleaned Lila up and brought her some food. She barely ate even now but had said was she suddenly hungry. As much as he wanted to see her eat, in the end, she hadn't touched a bite. Roan set the camera up on a tripod. He joined his wife and daughter. He kissed his wife as the camera flashed.

Soon the potion was cooling. All of the flower petals and gemstones were crushed into a fine powder. The gold-dust from the rings was added to the rainwater and Fae sugar. The last ingredient was one drop of placental blood. The liquid cooled down and turned a teal blue color. The strip of cloth was at the ready. Now the vigil would begin.

***

Blue candles were placed around the room, giving off a soft warm glow. The air smelled of lilac. The day was spent reminiscing and helping Lila to be comfortable. She was now unaware of her surroundings. Roan brought the little basket that Lila had thought was so sweet into the room and put his daughter into it. Juniper slept quietly. She hadn't truly cried yet. Already a good baby. Roan lay next to his wife's thin body. He gently cradled her, telling her that it was now okay for her to go, that soon she would be pain free and would never be ill again. "You'll be free. You'll soar and my love will be with you forever." Her breaths came in short gasps now. "It's okay, Baby. You've fought and won. I will be fine. I promise. The gift you've given me will always remind me of what a beautiful, brave and strong woman you are and forever shall be. I'll see you again. I promise. Soon, we'll all be together again. Now go. Fly. Baby fly!" Lila suddenly sat up. Her eyes were wide. She looked into the basket. Roan's heart leapt. He picked up the baby and brought her to Lila. She kissed the baby and Juniper's tiny eyes opened. She began wailing. Lila instantly smiled. She looked at Roan, her eyes suddenly bright and clear.

"I'm ready. I'm ready. I love you, Roan Francis Donovan. I'm ready." She fell back and the trio got to work. Each one carried the strip of green cloth and flew to Lila's head. Roan closed her eyes with his fingers, weeping. The trio placed the cloth over her eyes.

They waited and suddenly the room turned white. Blinding white. There was no noise. No movement. Just peace. It was done.

And I don't know what the future is holding in store
I don't know where I'm going, I'm not sure where I've been.
There's a spirit that guides me, a light that shines for me
My life is worth the living, I don't need to see the end.

Epilogue

Roan bit his lip as he watched Juniper put on her backpack. Her jumper was perfectly ironed and the dark green socks matched her green eyes. Her long auburn hair was braided and hung with little curls at the end. She picked up her sweater from the hook and pushed open the screen door. "Have a great day, Juni!" Roan kissed her. She hugged him.

"I will. See ya!" The school bus was waiting. She walked toward the porch steps and stopped. She slowly walked down the steps and looked in the grass by the garden gate. Seeing nothing, she shrugged and ran toward the bus. She stopped again and turned toward the house.

"Bye, Daddy! I love you!" He waved good-bye to her and sat on the steps. He watched her take her seat. As the bus drove away, a flash of blue appeared. Without looking around, Roan said aloud,

"Good morning, Lila." He took a deep breath. "Did you see her?" The hum of wings sounded behind him and Lila perched herself on a board of the white trellis that housed purple morning glories.

"I sure did."

"She was looking for you." he said casually. Sighing, Lila nodded.

"I saw. I'll catch up with her later. I can't believe she's in Kindergarten, Roan. She looked cute in her uniform." She sat under a blossom. Roan scooted his body back a few inches so he could see Lila. "You're doing a great job with her, Roan." She whispered then flew onto his shoulder. She kissed his cheek. She then flew back to her spot on the trellis. He nodded. He saw the trio loading herbs into the house by a lovely holly bush. He slapped his knee, smiling, and turned toward her.

"We both are."

The Beginning

www.ingramcontent.com/pod-product-compliance
Lightning Source LLC
Chambersburg PA
CBHW032155190626
46808CB00020B/381

* 9 7 8 0 6 1 5 8 1 7 3 7 8 *